# BOUND
# FOR MARS

Also by Arthur W. Ballou

MAROONED IN ORBIT

# BOUND
# FOR MARS

by Arthur W. Ballou

**LITTLE, BROWN AND COMPANY**
Boston · Toronto

*Published simultaneously in Canada*
*by Little, Brown & Company (Canada) Limited*

PRINTED IN THE UNITED STATES OF AMERICA

I am grateful to those from whose launching pad of factual knowledge and reasoned projections I have been permitted to take off with Colonel Sanborn and his fortunate company on their epic journey. I shall respect the desire of these modern Merlins to remain anonymous, the more so because I may have gone a step further, here and there, than they would consider justified.

A. W. B.

# BOUND
# FOR MARS

# 1

THE YOUNG PILOT of the rocket ferry peered out at the great glistening shape in front of him. Silhouetted against the darkness of outer space, it looked like a giant metal-spoked wheel. And the wheel was turning, revolving ponderously as it rolled along the invisible, endless turnpike of its polar orbit.

This was OFSET, his destination, the big inner-space station which was known in official terms as Orbital Facility for Space Exploratory Travel. Its more than three-hundred-foot diameter made it an impressive sight out in space.

Close by, its brand-new hull bright with reflected sunlight, rode a chunky cylinder. The pilot knew that this cylinder was not small — it measured eighty feet wide and one hundred and ten feet long — but it was effectively dwarfed by the great span of the space station. The cylinder was a spaceship. A flattened cone at one end marked its bow and a skeletal framework at the other end supported the thirty-three double-circle clusters of synthetic crystal emitters that would power and help to trim the craft in flight. OFSET was impressive-looking, but this other craft — as yet officially unnamed — had a mission that made the pilot stare hard at its strange outlines. In a few hours it would start for Mars.

The rocket ferry was closing rapidly on OFSET now, and the pilot turned his gaze back to his instruments. He was keeping a more than careful eye on the readout of ARDS, the Automatic Rendezvous and Docking System, this morning, for a part of his payload was wearing the uniform and insignia of a Terran Space Corps officer of high rank — the highest, in fact. General Everett Charles, Corps Commander, was on his way up to participate in the brief commissioning and takeoff ceremony that would mark the end of six years of preliminaries and the beginning of the longest journey in man's history.

As the shuttle craft eased in toward the docking facilities in OFSET's big hub, the General gazed across the quarter mile of space at the glistening new ship, a look of regret adding years to the stern lines of his face.

Once upon a very recent time he had been Colonel Charles, operational head of the MARSET project, with every hope and expectation of captaining this, man's first spacecraft big enough to be rightly called a ship. His would have been the challenge of leading an expedition across a hundred and fifty million miles of space, up the slope of solar gravity to Mars, there to establish a foothold for man. Fate, however, had decided otherwise. His predecessor had died, and he had been promoted. The General wore his stars without ostentation and carried his responsibilities without complaint, for he was that kind of man.

A younger man, tall and whipcord lean, now held the position of Colonel Commanding. Ike Sanborn had been the General's choice to head up MARSET, for he had worked on it from the beginning.

In the Commander's suite of the new interplanetary spaceship, Colonel Sanborn was signing the last papers for the last mail pouch before departure. His personal quarters were not lavish; the one eight-by-fourteen-foot room served as bedroom, office, and living room. It would take him a while, he thought now, to get used to it, to compress his living habits to fit the space.

Other of his habits had changed as well. He was aware of a new restriction in his relations with others, of a need to keep part of himself always uncommitted, always objectively ready to use the complete authority that was his alone. In the dangerous environment of deep space, each decision taken was a gamble, a gamble that the knowledge, experience, and sophistication of man would produce an answer acceptable under any conditions the environment might impose.

Prepared though he was to accept the loneliness of command, he welcomed with pleasure the news that the one man with whom he shared the load, General Charles, would be present at the brief formalities of commissioning. Not only would the visit give him personal enjoyment, it would also add a fillip of official recognition and dignity at a higher level of rank than Sanborn could supply. He looked at his watch. It was almost time.

The Colonel and his entire crew, both officers and men, were assembled in the control room when General Charles swung himself in around the doorjamb. All had braced themselves against the effects of weightlessness. They stiffened to attention, holding on tightly to keep themselves from drifting. The commissioning ceremony was under way.

By cutting the christening speech to little more than a bare announcement that the new ship would be known as the *Pegasus,* Sanborn's friend and executive officer, Major T. P. (Tip) Reagan, left the Colonel ample time to read his orders. The orders commissioned the ship and directed it to proceed to Mars's inner moon, Phobos, for a one-hour stopover, thence to the surface of the planet itself, there to establish and operate, until relieved, a permanent base for human habitation. For logistical reasons the present expedition would leave now to overtake Mars while it was still four months ahead of the Earth. All this Sanborn recited in a much more rapid manner than was customary for such weighty communications, thereby saving enough time for a few words from the General, who was ready and waiting.

"History affords few men the opportunity to achieve immortality," he began, the oratorical choice of words contrasting oddly with his curt manner of speaking. "Perhaps never before has a group of people been so certainly marked for a permanent place in the annals of man. This ship is most aptly named for Pegasus, the winged steed whose hoofs struck forth the fountain of inspiration from Helicon, the Mountain of the Sun, for —" the General paused for emphasis, "never before in history has mankind been inspired to unite so wholeheartedly in contributing resources and talent to a single, coordinated effort — of which you and your ship are both the result and the spearhead. The honor is a great one.

"So, too, is the responsibility. Years of painstaking labor and staggering amounts of material wealth are represented in this ship and its personnel. In your carefully chosen and trained hands rests the job of securing to mankind the best possible return on that great investment.

"Nothing will work more surely for you to that end than the homely blend of courage and enthusiasm known as 'high morale,' and nothing will magnify and multiply your inevitable difficulties as much as the lack of it. There is no doubt you will start off with it — don't ever lose it."

The General braced his weightless form solidly on his two feet by pushing upward on the walk-line gripped in his left hand. Drawing himself erect he concluded gruffly, "Gentlemen, I salute you. Godspeed, and a safe return."

He raised his right hand in a smart salute, held it for an instant, then pulled himself with awkward firmness to the door and left without a backward glance, amid a silence that was more of a sincere tribute than any applause. Ike Sanborn cleared his throat and spoke quietly.

"Some of you know that the man who just left has done more to make this project a reality than any other one person — and I say that from firsthand knowledge as officer in charge of Operation MARSET. If we attain immortality, as he put it, we can thank him for the opportunity." Turning to Reagan, whose blue-black eyes held a glint of approval, he said, "We get under way at 1100 hours. I shall accompany the General across to OFSET and be back aboard by 1045. Take charge until I return."

Without waiting for the tall, rangy Major's acknowledgment, Sanborn tugged on a handline and floated toward the doorway. There he braced himself and shoved off up the passage after General Charles with the smooth timing and economy of motion born of long familiarity. He hurried, knowing that one of OFSET's tenders was clinging barnaclelike to the personnel port of the launch compartment on B-deck, waiting to transport the General back to OFSET in time to catch the return rocket ferry down to space headquarters. Sanborn did not want the General to make that anticlimactic return to Earth without the thanks of the departing astronauts, for he was aware that Charles would have given almost anything to be one of them.

# 2

IKE SANBORN's familiarity with the General's feelings about *Pegasus* was solidly grounded. As a captain and later a major, he had served under the then Colonel Charles during the years of planning and development for the establishment of a colony on Mars. And a little over three years ago the Colonel had picked Sanborn to make a solo emergency flight to the Moon to rescue two fellow astronauts marooned in orbit there — a rescue whose narrow margin of success was made possible by the foresight and meticulous planning of its mission control officer, the same Colonel Charles. It was partly in recognition of his judgment and courage during the rescue that Sanborn had been made a lieutenant colonel and given acting charge of a part of Operation MARSET at that time.

For the next two years, over countless cups of coffee and hours of discussion, Ike Sanborn had come to know and to hold a deep regard for the wholly dedicated, rather lonely person that was Everett Charles, widower, father of an only daughter, and but recently a delighted grandfather. And in the continuous struggle to prepare for endless contingencies, to push, pull, needle and browbeat men and organizations into doing what must be done — right and on time — Sanborn learned from Charles the refined self-discipline and objective thinking with which his superior performed his seeming miracles of anticipation and planning.

When General Hart, Commander of the Terran Space Corps, retired, entered a hospital, and died, all within ten days, Everett Charles was the man picked to take over the job. Once installed, Charles yanked Sanborn upstairs to the rank of full colonel and gave him overall charge of Operation MARSET. After that the two men saw less of each other officially, though the new colonel was pleased to find that his commanding officer still welcomed the occasional shared meal that time allowed.

Now, during the moment it took him to reach the end of the passage, Sanborn was thinking of some of those less-formal times when the hard-bitten General had expressed quite human regret at his enforced separation from the day-to-day affairs of Operation MARSET. Charles must have known from the beginning, mused Sanborn, that his promotion to general automatically eliminated him from the present trip, to which he had been looking forward as a crowning achievement of his active-duty years.

A small red light in the frame of the air-lock door ahead went out and a smaller green one lighted up, signifying that the interlock was in neutral position and would permit the door to open as long as the one beyond it remained closed. The Colonel pushed hurriedly through the two doors into the main shaft, the long, gleaming tunnel that served as the ship's main stairwell and spinal column. Twelve feet across, the great tube was fashioned around a titanium alloy backbone from which sprouted successive layers of curved radial struts, four at each deck level. At each deck level, too, the glistening wall was interrupted by doors radiating out into the two or three airtight compartments into which the deck was divided. A narrow catwalk connected adjoining doors at each deck, running part way around the wall to give access to the up and down stairwells. The long array of spiral stairwells, struts, and doorways was so arranged as to leave two adjacent, unobstructed channels running the length of the ship, along which men and materials could move.

At the sound of the door closing behind Sanborn, the General looked back down the tunnel and a smile came over the stern lines of his face.

"It isn't necessary for you to see me off your ship, Commander. Mine was an informal visit, you know." His voice echoed in the shaft.

"Yes, sir, I know," responded Sanborn with a grin. "But you are the one who has made all this possible. I want to be sure that you know we appreciate what you have done for us — and for the mission. We don't run to bosun's pipes and side boys, but at least I can see you off the ship."

"Thank you, Colonel." Charles made no effort to hide his liking for the younger man. "I appreciate the courtesy and the thought behind it. Perhaps you would like to come over with me for a last word with Colonel Basso, if you have time. I know he would be pleased." Colonel Basso was commander of OFSET, which had served as bunkhouse and commissary during the assembly of the spaceship.

"I'd be glad to, sir," replied Sanborn quickly. "I was about to ask if you'd mind a passenger."

The General, arriving at the B-deck level, checked his drift and entered an air-lock door on which was stenciled L and R, standing for Launch and Recovery. Sanborn was close on his heels, and a moment later the two men were traversing the compartment toward the waiting tender.

"As familiar as all this is to me," said Charles, reflectively, "it looks very different now." His eyes roved about the room as they went. "I've been up here a dozen times, watching this ship evolve; I've been through it from stem to stern, seeing the things we planned take shape. But it was just so much hardware then. Now it's the real thing." The General paused at the open port and took a last quick look around. Then he slid quickly through and dropped into one of the tender's foam-lined contour seats.

"I know what you mean, sir," replied Sanborn, following. "The ship seems to have come alive these last few days, for all of us. Everyone is eager to get under way, and they're all beginning to call the ship 'she' instead of 'it.' You sensed it even in this very short visit."

"Ships do have personalities, Colonel," said Charles. "Oh, not rationally, of course, but somewhere back in a man's instinctive awareness he knows, the minute he steps aboard, whether a ship is good or bad, strong or weak."

Here the General paused to glance at their young pilot who was murmuring into his mike as the tender left the port with a smooth hiss, heading for the docking chamber in OFSET's hollow hub.

"This is nothing I'd expect to hear preached at Command Training School," he went on, with a little smile. "In fact I'd have to call it nonsense, for that's what it is, non-sense. But it's there all the same, and I'm glad yours is a good ship."

Then there was nothing more to say, but the silence was easy between them as the tender closed slowly on OFSET. In another minute magnetic grapples clanked on the stainless-steel shoe around the hatch, and the tender quivered. The teflon flange on the hatch fairing squeaked as hydraulic tongues locked the small craft in place.

# 3

As THE HATCH swung open, the first face they saw was that of Colonel Basso. He looked at Sanborn in worried surprise as the latter came aboard.

"Welcome back, sir," he said to the General quickly, then turned to Sanborn. "Nothing wrong, is there?" he asked.

"No, no, I just came over to quickly thank you again, Paul, for your help in these last months, for the practical suggestions that only you, with your experience in weightless environment, could have made. Besides which," Sanborn grinned, "you've always been ready to provide a sympathetic ear when I felt like blowing off steam."

Colonel Basso's brown eyes glowed beneath their

thick, black brows, and a momentary smile lighted up his normally saturnine features.

"It's been a privilege, Ike, believe me, to have a hand in your preparations. I'm grateful for the opportunity."

"Gentlemen," Sanborn held out his hand, "I must get back."

"Take this along." Basso produced a flat, oblong package as Ike started to turn away. "You'll understand. I'm sorry it's late."

"Thanks, Paul," responded Sanborn automatically, climbing into the tender. He read the pilot's name off the back of his shirt. "Let's go, Mister Senter." Then he settled back into the contour seat and raised a farewell hand to the two in the docking chamber.

What, he wondered, had Basso handed him?

Carefully he unwrapped the slender parcel, revealing a wafer-thin, oblong metal plate that had the soft patina of buffed silver with a hint of pale green in it. On it was a handsome gold likeness of the winged steed of Greek mythology for whom the new ship was named, poised in the act of springing from a crag. Beneath was a gold-lettered inscription bearing the name Pegasus, the date, and a three-line dedication:

TO THE OFFICERS AND MEN OF IPT *Pegasus*
FROM THE OFFICERS AND MEN OF OFSET
LUCIS PER ALA AD ASTRA

[ 1 7 ]

The plaque was a striking thing, the lettering austerely simple. Holding it between the outstretched fingers of both hands, Sanborn stared for a moment in admiration, tilting its shimmering surface this way and that to catch the light.

"What a handsome thing!" he thought. "We'll have to dream up something really distinctive to match that."

Gently rewrapping the plaque, Sanborn pulled out a small notebook and pencil and wrote himself a reminder.

"Idea contest for return gift to OFSET — later" it read. Replacing notebook and pencil in his shirt pocket, he glanced out the small, round window at his side.

To the right of their line of flight and slightly below it, a brilliant band of colors marked another sunset. Because their orbit girded the Earth almost sixteen times a day, at right angles to the sun's observed path, sunrise and sunset came so often they were taken for granted despite their vivid beauty. What would sunset look like on Mars, he wondered, where the atmosphere was only one percent the density of the Earth's, had almost no water vapor content, and was highly permeated with fine dust whirled aloft by the unceasing winds.

The black hulk of the *Pegasus* loomed up, blocking out an ever larger segment of star-flecked cosmos. The great, squat cylinder's true outlines were hinted at more than defined by slowly winking strobe lights on its hull, riding lights that made it visible to space traffic in the vicinity of OFSET. An occasional puff of vapor from an attitude control nozzle gleamed dazzling white in the intense beams. The personnel port, toward which they were heading, stood out in a little island of illumination provided by a small spotlight. Invisible were the bulbous nose and the after end with its power rings mounted on their spidery framework of struts and braces.

Colonel Sanborn craned forward, taking in all he could see of the spaceship's imposing bulk through the small craft's transparent nose. He could sense a stir of excitement deep within himself as the time for departure drew close. This voyage, though only a first step, was a goal toward which he had worked for years. Thousands of his own decisions had helped shape this dream that was about to become a reality, the first effort to plant a permanent colony on another planet.

In one of those flashes of speculative insight of which the human mind is occasionally capable, Sanborn saw himself and his companions as the embodiment of that restless, mysterious force which is the spirit of man, a force which had already carried man beyond his place of origin and showed no sign of lessening. It was a humbling experience.

The clink of grapples on the tender's hull recalled the Colonel to more immediate considerations. Picking up the plaque, he thanked the young pilot and slid through the hatchway into his ship, assisted by the hand of Lieutenant Amos Tandy, a compact, muscular member of Captain Larsen's Plant and Propulsion Section. Forestalling the other's greeting with a smile and a nod, he handed him the wrapped parcel.

"Have this put on my orderly's desk, Lieutenant," he said, moving away. A moment later he was passing through the air lock into the main shaft.

Entering the navigation compartment, or bridge, he saw Major Reagan lending a solicitous ear to something the Navigation Officer, Captain Frank Hewes, was saying.

". . . said he'd be back by 1045 hours and he is! Now why doesn't that man cast off and get out of here?"

Just then Reagan caught sight of the Commander and, tapping Hewes on the shoulder, jerked a big thumb toward the rear of the compartment.

"There he is," he said. "Why don't you ask him?"

"Port's closed, Captain!" Lieutenant McPhee, the stocky brown-haired young man at the master control console glanced over his shoulder toward Hewes and pointed to one of the half dozen twelve-inch viewers arrayed across the top of the console. On the screen was the outboard end of the L and R compartment, on which a small image of Tandy stood beside the tiny personnel port which was now closing.

The three in the back of the room turned their atten-

tion to the six-foot-square screen that served as a window
for the navigation compartment. It presented a three-
dimensional color reproduction of whatever was fed
into its circuits by either of the two basic scanning media
used by the *Pegasus*. It could "see" incoming energy
waves from infrared through ultraviolet and beyond, and
it could read out the return or reflection from anything
on which the ship's powerful scanners were trained.

At the moment the screen was filled with a view of
*Pegasus* herself, as seen by OFSET's scanners and
beamed over to the spaceship. As the three men watched,
a small bump detached itself from an illuminated spot
near the ship's nose and seemingly headed straight for
them, leaving a long white tail that swelled to bushy in-
distinctness and vanished. The tender that had brought
Colonel Sanborn was returning to OFSET, right into the
forefront of the scanner's field of view.

"Ready reports all in, Captain?" inquired Sanborn.

"Yes, sir. All hands at takeoff stations," replied Hewes.

"Good. Major, will you continue in charge?"

Without waiting for Reagan's reply, Sanborn grasped
a handline and pulled himself across the room to where
he could watch Lieutenant McPhee working his system-
atic way to the bottom of a long check-off sheet, and at
the same time keep an eye on the systems monitoring
panels of the console. Some of these panels glowed with
clusters of little green cat's-eyes, staring or winking out

their messages of reassurance. Others showed only small dark holes from which red warnings would gleam if something went wrong.

Behind the Master Console, in a transparent-walled cubicle that was always kept at an air-conditioned seventy degrees and thirty percent humidity, lived Nan, the computer, so-called because she performed the individual steps of her occult routine in nanoseconds, or billionths of a second. Nan was one of the very latest offspring of the computer tribe, with an efficiency of size, capacity, and speed that made her ancestors seem as antique as the bow and arrow. Minute, integrated chip circuitry and the latest techniques of data compression and differentiation enabled Nan to run things from an area not much bigger than a coat closet. If Nan became incapacitated, her not-so-smart sister who lived on D-deck could run the vital functions connected with navigation and life support. This back-up computer inhabited a lead-lined cell to protect it against radiation that might damage its information storage, which was a complete duplicate of Nan's and was updated constantly. "Second storage," as it was called, insured that one or the other computer would always have access to the data needed to carry on its functions.

Above McPhee's head, white figures rolled past the square windows of the day-clock, indicating seven minutes to departure time. Below was a row of eight similar windows, each one showing a white zero. At precisely 1100 hours, the right-hand window of this elapsed mission time chronometer would begin to show movement as the instrument started its monotonous, meticulous chronicle of seconds, minutes, and hours.

Sanborn had decided several days earlier that Tip Reagan would be in operational command at the time of takeoff. He wanted to keep himself unencumbered, to watch, listen, get the feel of this crew and ship. All but a few of the expedition's members were Space Corps personnel, some with active-service backgrounds. The others, together with those who did not belong to the corps, had special competence in some scientific discipline bearing on the mission. Their lack of active-duty training and experience had been largely compensated for by a series of special classes. Everyone had to help man the ship — space and weight were too precious for it to be otherwise. At the other end, too, each would have to perform a part of the task of establishing a foothold on the windswept, dusty surface of Mars.

Waiting for the final minutes and seconds to spin by, Sanborn was conscious of an odd, detached feeling, as if he were in reality two people. One hung there behind McPhee, watching and listening. The other, a shadowy extrasensory awareness, focused on the other preparations being made throughout the ship for the moment when the Kresch drive would stab the purple darkness outside with its megawatts of converted actinic energy, brighter than the sun's distant eye and just as soundless.

Waiting time was down to five minutes now, and the nine mass converters in the spaceship's shielded tail section were being brought up to operating level. The Colonel's eye caught the first upward flicker of the gauges as internal shielding was slowly withdrawn, exposing more reactive mass to the growing storm of nuclear particles in the CN reactors which took matter apart and liberated the tremendous amounts of energy required to keep the complex actinic drive in operation. For an instant Sanborn's shadow-self took control, and he was aft with the power plant in that almost soundless compartment where rows of strange metallic shapes made energy from matter in a continuous, fully automatic cycle. Only the intermittent hum and whine of servo-mechanisms tending their hidden nuclear fires broke the stillness in the big cylindrical chamber.

Then the logical sector of the Commander's mind took charge again, and the power plant dwindled to a set of symbols on one panel of the master console. A bit more than four minutes remained before departure. Sanborn, whose residual momentum had allowed him to drift into an almost head-down position, pushed gently with one foot against the overhead as if to tiptoe across it, holding fast meanwhile to a handline. He pivoted slowly around to land upright on both feet. After three months of weightless living, the maneuver came as naturally as one rising from a sitting position. For the same reason Sanborn's gyration attracted no notice from the others. A person's position relative to floors and ceilings had been a matter of chance and preference long enough to dull the novelty of seeing people dangling about at odd angles.

Captain Finberg, the expedition's medical officer, had been the first to comment on one possible and very interesting effect of their extended stay in a weightless environment.

"Think of the countless gravity-affected modes of thought, speech, and action a man acquires," he had said a few nights earlier as they sat at dinner aboard OFSET, relaxing in the comfortable grip of its spin-induced centrifugal force. "From the moment he begins to lift his head to listen and look around — when he learns what 'stand up' and 'fall down' mean — as his reflexes become conditioned to the task of keeping him upright, whether standing or moving, in response to certain kinds of visual evidence plus certain sensations originating in the organs of the inner ear and certain other sensations of various balancing muscles — and when he becomes aware, at least subconsciously, that the vertical dimension of his world is inextricably linked up with the force we call 'gravity' — do you see what I'm getting at? By the time he has passed infancy, the habit of gravity is as much a part of him as the habit of breathing. And yet" — Finberg's eyes glowed — "here are we, after less than three months' intermittent exposure to a weightless environment, quite successfully adapted to a world in which the force of gravity has no empiric reality.

"If man's senses, created and conditioned exclusively on Earth, are capable of such a complete switch, and his mind is capable of reprogramming itself to function normally under a totally foreign set of sensory stimuli," concluded Finberg, "we are better prepared for the trip because we have had this time to free ourselves of standard gravity thought patterns and reflexes."

"What you're telling us, Captain," said Major Cardoza, head of the expedition's bionics section, with a smile, "is that we are lucky to have had time to get used to it. Right?"

Finberg's darkly handsome features relaxed in a grin.

"Yes, sir, that, and we're lucky we do get used to it. We seem to be better designed than we suspected."

# 4

THE DAY-CLOCK above McPhee's head showed but two minutes remaining before takeoff, the actual split-second timing of which would be controlled by the computer. Nan had been in primary control of some functions for as much as forty-eight hours, running the direct life-support systems and linking up its complex navigation programs and stored data with actual live input from the inertial and astral components of the on-board system and with information from OFSET, whose absolute position, course, altitude, and velocity, as related to Earth, were always known.

There was provision for human interruption of the takeoff sequence, of course, and a very few abort options in the automated program itself to cover things such as a massive reactor or propulsion failure or a major impairment of structural integrity. Anything less would have to be handled under way, for there were ninety-six unmanned, actinic-powered cargo carriers drifting slowly around the Earth far out in space, in an orbit whose plane lay along the path to be followed by *Pegasus*. *Pegasus* was to rendezvous with these cargo sleds and lead them to Mars. Already accelerating in their elliptical orbit, the eight dozen flattened cones formed a giant cone. The spaceship must arrive at the tip of that cone at the precise instant when its path and theirs could be joined within the narrow "window" that led to a successful Martian transit course. Failure to accomplish the rendezvous would cost the expedition eight days of lost time, waiting for the next workable combination of orbits and "window" to come along and making up in extra travel for the alteration in their escape and transit courses.

"T minus one minute and running," announced Lieutenant McPhee with just a shade more emphasis than he usually permitted himself.

Captain Hewes, the Navigation Officer, had come up beside Sanborn, while big Tip Reagan continued to hold onto a corner of the cargo carrier monitor near the back of the room. The center of attention at this critical time was the control console. The curving, ten-foot array of switches, buttons, knobs, dials, and lights was almost fully activated now; only the acceleration and actinic power gauges were resting on zero.

Again McPhee spoke, starting the traditional thirty-second countdown whose end would mark the beginning of a new era in man's territorial aspirations.

Sanborn wondered if any of the others were prey to the tension that each of McPhee's words seemed to screw a notch tighter.

"T minus twenty-five — T minus twenty —"

Captain Hewes found himself gnawing the inside of his lower lip, and he envied the Commander's cool self-possession.

"T minus fifteen — T minus ten, nine, eight —"

The fingers of Reagan's big, hairy hand were white with the strength of his grip on the Cargo Carrier Monitor, but neither he nor anyone else was aware of it.

"Three, two, one — acceleration, posigrade, begun at T plus two hundred and forty milliseconds."

For the space of a heartbeat nothing seemed to be happening. Sanborn heard his own heart thump.

Then, with infinite gentleness, the floor pressed on the soles of his feet, and a soft, creaking stir passed through the ship as its bearing members and surfaces took up the load of its own mass plus that of men, supplies, and equipment.

They were under way.

The first apparent effect of the gentle acceleration was the restoration of weight to the *Pegasus* and her contents, weight at one-twentieth normal because the acceleration was only one-twentieth of a standard gravity. The fact that this newly acquired weight was at right angles to the Earth's surface and was a function of acceleration rather than gravitation did not change its effect. Once again it would be possible to sit down, lie down, put things down. Food could be served on a plate, and a glass of water could be poured out and handled without the risk of its erupting into a cloud of liquid fragments at the slightest jar. But this new gravity was a tenuous, slow-motion sort of thing. A quick movement would vanquish it temporarily, and an impatient step would propel the stepper forward and upward in a lazy, looping bound that was likely to thump his head or hand on the ceiling.

Other, more immediate concerns had to do with the effect of gravity on the *Pegasus* herself and on the stores and equipment she carried.

Down on E-deck, at the ship's center of mass, the inertial devices that gauged acceleration, attitude, and any aberrant motion were watched over critically by two men, of whom the shorter, slimmer one wore the higher rank. Benjamin Marcus, the expedition's astrophysical specialist, had the crew-cut look of an undergraduate, but he wore a colonel's pip beside the armillary-sphere-and-atom insignia on the collar of his pale-blue shirt, and there was nothing immature about his full-lipped, rather petulant mouth and the cool self-assurance of his dark eyes.

As the moment of takeoff arrived and passed, Colonel Marcus watched with unwavering attention the slow, even buildup of acceleration that would stabilize presently at a foot and a half per second, held there by delicate inertial controls regulating the Kresch drive's variable power output.

Close by, stocky, red-haired John Pryor, whose collar bore the wheel and star of navigation, was equally attentive to the attitude and displacement gauges. The small gold V on the upper arm of his shirt denoted the rank of chief technician and marked him as qualified to both handle and service the complex equipment.

They were there in the inertial guidance compartment to provide immediate theoretical and practical help and advice in the unlikely event of a malfunction. The equipment they were watching so closely was the source of one of the two sets of navigational data necessary for a successful rendezvous with the red planet. Called INS input, this Inertial Navigation System data fed continuously into the computer's navigation channel, along with the ANS input of data gathered by the Astral Navigation System. A visual composite of either system, or both, could be projected onto one of the master control console's multi-purpose screens, together with a third point of light representing perfect compliance with the desired course.

# 5

NOT ALL the small work parties stationed here and there throughout the ship were precautionary, as were Marcus and Pryor. Most of them had specific tasks to perform.

In the L and R section of B-deck, Lieutenant Amos Tandy and three men of the plant and propulsion section were spaced at equal intervals along the length of the room, their backs to the four teardrop-shaped auxiliary craft anchored along the left-hand wall. Before them was the on-board supply of repair and maintenance parts for the auxiliary craft, the cargo carriers, and some portions of *Pegasus* herself, all stored in a series of what seemed dangerously light plastic bays, bins, shelves, and trays. Actually the featherweight storage receptacles were fully adequate under conditions where a ten-pound rocket nozzle weighed but eight ounces and a solid little four-pound quartz gyro unit accounted for just over three ounces. Larger items were fitted or fastened in place, but the smaller ones were stored loose in their trays, confined only by gossamer-thin sheets of transparent plastic in flip-cover frames. A largely concealed lithium alloy skeleton ran through the rows of receptacles, emerging vertically at intervals from the top of each unit in slim, silvery rods that fastened to the ceiling.

The squad's initial assignment was to be sure that nothing bounced or slid out of its appointed place when acceleration began. Directly in front of the curving rows waited George Foran and Harry Cohen. The former was a gangling young man whose bony features wore a constant, determinedly blasé expression that failed to conceal his joy at being aboard. Cohen, a few years older, had the stocky, full-muscled figure of physical maturity, capped by a thick brush of dark-red hair with brows to match. Hard, brown eyes, big lips, and a large nose gave him a tough look at first glance.

At the inner end of the line, to Cohen's right, stood big Ed Mayer, whose placid manner and large frame lent him a quite erroneous air of slow clumsiness. His assignment, like that of Lieutenant Tandy at the far end, was an airtight closet of large pressure cylinders. At Mayer's end the cylinders were orange and contained rocket fuel. Green ones full of oxidizer filled the other small chamber. For safety the two closets were separated by the full length of the compartment, their doors controlled by an interlock so that only one could be open at a time. A small, shielded inspection plate was set into each door and a gas analyzer occupied a niche in each closet.

Once the inspection was complete the men would cross the compartment to where the four A-Cs (auxiliary craft) hung in their preflight fastenings, waiting to be released and readied for use. Most of this job would be handled by two men, but all four would help transfer each craft to a launching skid and secure it in standby position.

Now, as McPhee's countdown rasped from the overhead speaker, Tandy and Mayer moved up to their peepholes. Mayer, with his great height, merely reached one hand to the ceiling and braced his feet on the floor. The shorter Lieutenant used the door handle to hold himself in position. As McPhee began the final, second-by-second count, even Cohen, who fancied himself the expedition's keenest wit, was silent.

"— three, two, one — acceleration —"

As the terse recital ended, there was an instant of absolute quiet, then a clicking, rustling sound as thousands of items, big and little, sought a stable equilibrium in their appointed places.

"We're moving!"

The low exclamation came from George Foran, who followed it up with an ears-and-all blush at the sound of his own excited voice.

"You can still make it, George!" called Cohen in mock urgency. "Get on a pressure suit, quick, and we'll shove you out the air lock! Somebody's bound to notice you sooner or later."

"Save the comedy, Cohen, and keep your eyes on the job," broke in Lieutenant Tandy firmly, but with a quirk on his own lips.

"Yes, sir," replied Cohen with that touch of brashness that just escapes rudeness and is used by the professional enlisted man for testing the mettle of junior officers.

Tandy demonstrated his competence by ignoring all but the letter of Cohen's acknowledgment. Instead, he addressed a brief order to both Foran and Cohen.

"Carry on with your inspections."

Putting his eye to the inspection glass once more, he took a final look at the motionless stand of man-high pressure flasks, thinking again how convenient it had been to have the four-hundred-pound brutes weightless during loading. Even now they weighed but twenty pounds apiece in the form of inertial resistance to the ship's steady, mild acceleration. Satisfied that the oxidant cylinders were all right for the moment, he moved toward the nearest aisle of storage bins to help Foran and Cohen complete their task.

"Fuel locker looks OK, sir," called Mayer from the far end of the compartment. "I'll start on the bins."

"All right," replied Tandy, regarding with amused envy the ease with which the big fellow placed a casual hand on the ceiling to give himself the stability and traction required for rapid movement. Only one other man, Major Reagan, had the height and reach to do that. The rest, himself included, had to move about somewhat in the manner of a sleepwalker without the outstretched arms, at least until they could reach a wall or other rigid surface from which to shove off. With practice, it was possible to ricochet along at better than walking speed, using a long, tiptoeing stride, provided one did not try to stop or turn quickly without a hand assist.

"Anyone find anything loose?" Tandy looked at the three in turn as they assembled in front of the storage racks.

No one had.

"All right. Cohen and Mayer, check out the suit locker while Foran and I go over the oxidant flasks. Come back here when you finish. You can do the fuel locker while we strip out handlines and tiedowns."

As the first two left for the small adjoining chamber where pressure suits and helmets were kept, the voice of

[3 7]

Lieutenant McPhee grated from the intercom with that harsh, metallic ring favored by the designers of public address systems because its penetrating sharpness assures attention.

"Launch room party, report your status."

"First inspection complete and all OK, David," responded Tandy, his voice caught and transmitted by one of the sensitive microphones overhead. "We're about to start on the cylinders and suit locker. Then we'll go to the A-Cs."

"Good. Call in from quarters when you get there. Out."

The speaker clicked off on McPhee's reference to their final takeoff assignment, a check of the living quarters that occupied the rest of B-deck.

"All right, Mister Foran, let's make sure these oxidant cylinders are secure," said Tandy, opening the door of the narrow closet.

# 6

IN A SMALL COMPARTMENT on F-deck, illuminated only by red light reminiscent of a photographic
darkroom, a thick-set, heavy figure lurked motionless at
one end of a narrow aisle. Major Ralph Cardoza, the expedition's chief bionics officer, was a solid man of medium
height when viewed in broad daylight; here in the dull
red glow of the algae irradiation chamber, he was a gross
and sinister shape brooding over a devil's distillery.

Along both sides of the narrow room ran parallel
banks of shallow, sealed trays through which flowed the
several types of algae comprising the heart of the ship's
life-support system. Here infrared radiation, in differing
amounts for the various types of algae, provided the
energy used by the algae to grow and multiply and to

feed on the different blends of slurry in which they lived and rode, pumped from slurry tank to irradiator to separator and back to slurry tank in a continuous cycle.

This complex and delicate operation was known as a closed life-support system because it made use of the algae's ability to consume human wastes and produce human requirements. Through the magic of photosynthesis, powered by the infrared radiation, the chlorophyll-rich algae used slurry and $CO_2$ from stale air to produce the fats, proteins, vitamins and hormones, and oxygen needed by the crew. Together with purified water obtained as a by-product of the slurry preparation, these products fulfilled the human requirements of breathing, drinking, washing, and eating.

The crew's diet would be supplemented by a variety of dehydrated natural foods, more for esthetic considerations of texture and composition than for any lack of flavor or nutritional values. The algae were subjected to a battery of seasonings and flavorings as well as handling techniques such as compression and dehydration. From them could be prepared dishes simulating various meats, vegetables, and starches, as well as bread, rolls, and cake with fruit sauces. Compared bite for bite with the genuine article, each was detectably different, but in no case was the taste objectionable, and the synthetic foods were nutritionally better balanced.

Salt, to which the algae were not partial, was also a

by-product of the cycle, but sugar and dehydrated coffee, tea, eggs, and milk were carried as dietary supplements.

There was more, of course, to the life-support system than the algae cycle, for the purified water and oxygen-enriched, humidified air had to be circulated throughout the ship, and a satisfactory living temperature maintained. These functions were essentially mechanical, even if some of the regulating and sensing devices were electronically activated. The effect of the ship's increased gravity on these subsystems was simply to increase the amount of work performed, to compensate for the newly acquired weight of the air and water.

In the case of the algae cycle, however, the gravity upon acceleration introduced a number of complications. One was the tendency of the various mixes to separate or stratify into solid, liquid, and gaseous fractions. This was an advantage at that point in the cycle where algae and refreshed air were removed, but it constituted an unacceptable handicap in the growth and irradiation phases. A blender in each system could overcome the difficulty in large measure, but algae are temperamental, and a well-behaved strain, exposed to new conditions, might possibly decide to slow its growth rate or even die.

With this in mind, Major Cardoza had stationed himself beside the panel of instruments and repeaters in the irradiation chamber. There he could follow the two main criteria of the algae's well-being — their oxygen output

[ 41 ]

and their rate of multiplication — during the critical time immediately following the start of acceleration. There, too, he could verify the occurrence of certain changes programmed to take place automatically, such as slight increases in circulating and blending pump speeds and in gas pressure. And only there could he make the one change deliberately left to be done by hand, the adjustment of sliding shields on the irradiation trays to vary the exposure.

The optimum amount of irradiation varied from batch to batch of algae, even from the same strain, and the Major was dealing with all new batches comprised of several strains. If a batch perished, the dead mix had to be dumped into the ship's waste tank, the system sterilized and charged with new slurry, and a small batch of the desired strain of algae introduced and nursed into full bloom — a two- or three-day job during which the life-support system was not self-sustaining, and precious supplies of oxygen and chemicals would have to be used to make up the difference.

McPhee's countdown, followed by the faint nudge of the floor against Cardoza's feet, blanked out his awareness of everything but the hooded glow of the instruments. As he watched, the oxygen-carbon dioxide–ratio fell slowly in each of the systems, and in each the viscosity sensor registered increased stratification, thinner at the top and thicker at the bottom. These initial physical reactions to acceleration were expected. They ought to reverse their direction and return to normal within a couple of minutes, particularly the tendency toward separation. The blending and circulating pumps had increased their faint hum as more power was applied automatically to counteract the separation.

Standing there alone in the red dusk of the chamber, the Major found himself actively willing his several billion microscopic laborers to work harder, as if they were indeed tiny rational beings who would respond to the impact of his thought waves.

"In a way," he thought, "I am God as far as these little organisms are concerned, the unsensed manipulator of their heredity and environment, with resources and means at my command that are infinitely beyond their simple, eat-and-multiply level of existence."

Turning the thought over in his mind, he wondered if it had a parallel in the relation between his own level of existence and whatever it was that controlled the universe. Like many of his contemporaries, Ralph Cardoza had no particular faith in the religious sense; he believed rather that there was no secret too small, no concept too vast, to be beyond the eventual reach of man's intellect. Now, for an instant, he wondered.

The viscosity readings began to converge on normal, reflecting the increased turbulence and consequent smoother mixture in tanks and lines as the slurries responded to the increased thrust of the pumps. Oxygen production, too, had stopped falling in all but one system.

Cardoza propelled himself in a flat-footed shuffle to the nearest rack of irradiation trays and began the task of resetting the sliding covers, a task that would occupy him for the next two to three hours.

Similarly throughout the *Pegasus,* wherever the advent of acceleration, with its reciprocal "gravity," called for attention, men were busy. Every man aboard had an assignment in this first step of their journey up the flattening slope of Earth's gravitational pull.

Slowly the velocity climbed, each second putting behind them a foot and a half more than its predecessor. At the end of 3600 seconds, or one hour, for example, *Pegasus* had added 5400 feet per second — more than a mile a second — to the circular velocity at which she had been born, 25,000 miles per hour. Increasing centrifugal force built up by the growing speed gradually changed the ship's circular orbit into an expanding spiral, thus slowly beginning their actual outward acceleration. As thrust continued and the ship got further away from the Earth, the effect of its gravity diminished more quickly and the course veered more and more away from the circular. At the preselected time and place, their expanding spiral intersected the path of the cargo sleds, and the

*Pegasus* took over their guidance. Shortly afterward, escape velocity was attained; they were under way.

Most of the crew were newcomers to ultralunar space, had never been beyond the Moon, though all had the required cislunar time, even the "rebrands," like Captain Larsen, who had been picked for the expedition because they possessed special talents and who were civilians in normal life. As the first hours became a day and off-duty time became available, most of these men found an opportunity to stargaze at the incomparable beauty of their home planet, a spherical wonder of incredibly pure blue and white swirls, gradually dwindling in the purple velvet of space. The Moon, eclipsed initially by its shimmering big sister, showed up as a pallid white echo on the second day, as their first million miles fell behind. By the end of the third day, as they neared the five-million-mile mark and their velocity crept up over a quarter million miles per hour, the Moon had shrunk to a seed pearl that appeared to rest on one edge of its brilliant companion.

Day and night were completely arbitrary in their little world, as to all intents and purposes were speed and distance. There were no alternating periods of light and darkness outside. Nor were there mileposts to verify the fact that they were slashing through space so fast that the mileposts themselves would have blended into a solid rail flowing past at more than seventy-five posts per second. Theirs was a curiously intellectual, rather than sensory, awareness that they were bound out across interplanetary space along a hyperbolic path bent slightly this way and that by the pull of the sun and planets, but leading at last to Phobos and Mars.

# 7

THE HUMAN SKILLS required in an undertaking such as this one dictated a level of education and training considerably above average. This in turn meant that there were far more chiefs than Indians in the makeup of the crew of the *Pegasus*. A high level of automation had eliminated much of the routine work formerly done by human minds and hands.

There remained those jobs, largely service and maintenance, for which a lesser degree of reason, judgment, and training was required. In terms of man-days of work, these tasks called for ten or twelve technically competent but not necessarily highly educated men. In practice, however, the actual number was reduced to four. Most of the younger members of the expedition would not have a full load of duties until they reached the immediate vicinity or the surface of Mars, and so their spare time was put to use in filling out the shipboard duty roster.

Only the holographic memory of the Terran Space Corps personnel computer knew how many technicians and "noncoms" had applied when the word went out that four men would be chosen competitively from the corps to make the trip. Names and serial numbers were still coming in a month after the closing date. From nearly eight thousand volunteers who got in under the wire, sixty-four were chosen and detached from their regular units for extensive testing and training, during which time their number was further reduced to the sixteen who were eventually selected to complete the training. Of these sixteen, four were finally named to the crew. The others, designated as first, second, and third alternates, were assigned to supporting duties that enabled them to undergo the same indoctrination and conditioning as the lucky four.

Thus it happened that First Alternate George Foran had been able to move up with confidence into the vacancy created less than a week before departure by the sudden eruption of crewman Hans Ling's appendix.

Young Foran, as everyone called him, had cultivated a sober, thoughtful expression to lend an air of maturity to his long, narrow schoolboy face. With a factual mind and a retentive memory, George had the potential to go far in some one of the sciences and indeed had made no little progress in communications photonics school since entering the corps.

Selected to try out for a place on the expedition's roster, Foran drove himself unmercifully to excel in all phases of the competitive training and testing. He very much wanted a place in the first four. When notified that he had been selected as a first alternate, he very nearly went AWOL and his sober expression took on a tinge of bitterness.

Then came the astounding news of his last-minute reprieve, and though he did manage to look and feel sympathetic toward his predecessor when they parted, it was an effort.

Even now, ten days out, his brows would lift every so often, and a look of wonder would sweep across his face, and he would look about him as if to be sure that his incredible good fortune was an actuality and not an illusion.

George was seated before the cargo carrier monitor, a combination tracking and telemetry device atop a flaring base near the rear of the control room. The monitor was the only watch station in the control room to which anyone other than navigation department personnel was ever posted, and then only during certain hours of the day. Its operator had the intentionally simple duty of relaying to the watch officer the locator number and bearings of any cargo sled that strayed off station more than five degrees or five hundred yards. The monitor would emit an audio-visual warning under those conditions, so the person on duty was free to gaze to his heart's content at the hundreds of lights and dozens of instrument clusters in the master control console, or to stare, bemused, at the big video screen on which was usually displayed a wide-angle view of the heavens ahead, re-created with a breathtaking three-dimensional fidelity that made the six-foot square look like an open window.

Since the likelihood of a cargo sled getting far enough off course to trigger the alarm was something like one in a hundred thousand, the monitor watch assignment was in effect an official opportunity to do what was otherwise forbidden, to sight-see in the control room. Captain Hewes, the otherwise affable head of navigation, had been quite explicit about sightseers visiting his control room.

"If your duties take you there, be there," was how he put it. "If not, keep out. We've all spent the last three months up here putting this craft together and equipping her and everyone knows pretty well what she looks like from stem to stern. You'll all have occasion to be on the bridge now and then."

Remembering, George was surprised to realize that nearly two weeks had gone by since Captain Hewes had delivered his edict to the crew at one of the after-dinner briefing sessions aboard OFSET, their globe-girdling construction base. True to his word, the Captain had arranged for split-shift watches at the monitor to give everyone a chance to see the fascinating spectacle presented by the control room of an interplanetary spaceship under way.

From where he sat George could see the entire semicircular compartment by swiveling his chair in a half circle. To his far left was the transparent, dust-proof cubicle that housed the ship's main computer center. Next came the long, curving master control console with its banked rows of manual switches, dials and selectors, its clusters of meters, gauges, and lights, large and small, steady and pulsating, spelling out the welfare and performance of the *Pegasus* at a glance.

To the right of the console, and beyond it, the gleaming, six-foot-square main viewer dominated the forward center of the room, a magic window on the star-studded vastness through which they swept. To the right again, and opposite the master console, there stood a smaller array of instrumentation clusters, the subsidiary and auxiliary systems console, before which sat the muscular, square-jawed, red-haired figure of Navigation Technician John Pryor, his shoulders back, close-cropped head erect, in that exaggerated-looking posture that is in reality the most restful position for sedentary vigilance.

The departmental file and emergency small-stores lockers came next, taking up the remaining space be-

tween Pryor's station and the survival unit in the right
hand corner, where pressure suits, food, water, a chemical toilet, and a recharging tank for oxygen flasks were
stored. The survival unit would make possible life and
continuing control of the ship for sixteen man-days
should an accident isolate the bridge from the rest of
*Pegasus,* or in the event of sudden decompression.
Though the latter possibility was about as remote as
Antares, all the systems in the control room were designed, tested, and installed to operate in vacuo, including
a double-acting pressure relief valve in the airtight cell
that housed the computer. Even the hermetically sealed
glass sandwich that was the main view screen had been
tested in a vacuum chamber in which the ambient pressure had been held for one week at one-hundreth of a
picotorr, or one hundred-trillionth of one-seven hundred
sixtieth of a standard atmosphere, in rough simulation of
the vacuum of space.

The first half hour of this, Foran's second monitor
watch, had passed in what seemed like five minutes as
he found himself entranced anew by the hypnotic glow
and wink of the many lights in the upper panels of both
consoles, and by the eerie, sharper-than-life reality of
the slightly magnified image of the path ahead. The
screen was a hole of purple darkness in which there
glittered a few big diamond-sharp stars that looked

relatively near, along with a host of others, some sharp, some fuzzy, dwindling away like luminous grains of sand. Fascinating though the intricacies of the consoles were, it was to the awesome spectacle of the cosmos that Foran's eyes came back time and again.

# 8

THE DRY BUZZ of the monitor's alert signal failed to penetrate George's concentration for a second or two. His sudden awareness of it coincided with a sharp query from the stocky, dark-haired watch officer seated at the master control console.

"What's happening there, Foran?" Lieutenant Munn spun his contour chair half around and stared impatiently.

"One of the cargo carriers seems to be having trouble, sir," replied Foran stiffly, feeling the hot blood rush to his cheeks. "Number L-5 is red-lighted."

"Seems to be!" the Lieutenant snorted, dark eyes hard. "If you're sure it is only L-5, let me have the coordinates, quick!"

"It is just L-5 sir." George confirmed his statement with a careful glance, resenting the other's abruptness and angry at himself for muffing the alert signal. "Bearings 118.4 by 19.3." He bit his tongue to keep from adding a second, egregious "sir" to his reply. It was not, after all, Lieutenant Munn's fault that he'd been slow to respond.

Munn moved with swift competence, speaking the big scanner screen's access code and the two bearings into the computer microphone, then turning to Pryor:

"Mister Pryor, get me a readout on carrier L-5's telemetry."

"Working on it now, sir," responded John Pryor, who had been a silent witness to the sharp exchange between his watchmates. He moved in a single, slow-motion bound to the monitor pedestal and punched a series of numbers into the keyboard beside the screen. As he finished, the neat rows of blips representing ninety-six unmanned cargo sleds trailing after them through space vanished from the screen to be replaced by a picture of an instrument cluster similar to that of the generator-propulsion group in the small, Ray-class ships. The pictured instruments had no real existence aboard the cargo carrier; they were concocted by the computer's program for telemetry readout to give meaning to the glowing dots and lines produced on the screen by the actual data from the sled.

[55]

"I have it on screen, sir. Do you want a split?" Pryor spoke quickly, one finger poised over the button that would reproduce the image before him in one corner of the big scanner at which Lieutenant Munn was staring.

"Hold it a minute." Munn fiddled with a knob beneath the screen, watching a slowly contracting white blur that hovered a little to one side of center for a moment, then gradually drifted in, resolving as it did into the sharp image of a carrier. A few seconds later, however, it sagged back to its original position, dwindling as it did to a fuzzy white wafer.

"OK, split it," said Munn abruptly, then spoke into the intercom. "Captain Hewes, Bridge calling Captain Hewes."

Pryor spoke, low voiced, in the ensuing silence. "Look at the main voltage, sir. It was off for about ninety seconds —"

"This is Captain Hewes," came the voice of their superior in his pleasant, rather flat accents. "What is it, Lieutenant?"

"Will you come to the bridge, sir? We have a malfunction in one of the cargo sleds. Tracking and voltage are irregular."

"I'll be right there. Ask Colonel Sanborn to come up if he is free." The Captain's accent was noticeably flatter, and his words came from the speaker in a staccato burst.

Obediently Lieutenant Munn put in a call for the Colonel.

"The Commander is with Major Cardoza, sir, in the algae compartment, E-deck." The voice was that of Sanborn and Reagan's office staff, a chubby technician named Cy Rowe. "Major Reagan is on deck if —"

"Thank you Mister Rowe, I'll reach the Colonel there," broke in Munn, confident that both Hewes and Sanborn would want it so. He switched to the algae compartment's line, got the Colonel on the phone, and passed on Hewe's request, outlining the situation that prompted it.

"Tell Captain Hewes I'll be there at once, and look up the cargo on L-5," was Sanborn's crisp reply, almost before Munn stopped speaking, and again the line clicked off.

Captain Frank Hewes pushed through the air lock and propelled himself toward the master control console with a one-handed shove off the wall and a long, tiptoeing stride that seemed barely to brush the deck, so little did he weigh in the ship's low-gravity environment. Reaching the console, he arrested his progress by grasping the back of the navigator's seat and proceeded to stare intently at the scanner.

"The readout is good on everything up to the laser pumps, sir," volunteered Pryor from the supply train monitor, after a moment's silence.

The Captain isn't blind, you fool, thought Munn,

checking a surge of impatience. Aloud he said, "What is the cargo aboard L-5, Mister Pryor?"

Normally that information would have been obtained by a query in the form of numbers punched into the monitor's keyboard, and the answer would have appeared on the screen. But now the screen was taken up with the instrument readout, and that could not be "erased" without simultaneously erasing the duplicate of it on the big screen, at which Captain Hewes was looking. Munn knew that and knew that Pryor knew it too, and he expected and intended to keep the latter busy for several minutes looking up the information in the cargo manifest file. He was amazed, therefore, when Pryor replied without the slightest hesitation.

"Metal and plastic hardware for the hydroponic station, sir."

Munn, who knew that the other had not had the time or the occasion to get the information in advance, searched in vain for any indication of levity in Pryor's manner.

"How do you know that, Mister?" he asked skeptically.

"I've memorized the cargoes, sir. I have a trick memory," responded the stocky redhead without offense.

Just then the airlock swung open again to admit the tall, lean figure of Colonel Sanborn. The others moved aside as he crossed to the scanner and stood frowning at it intently, marking the rise and fall of the sled's main voltage, the intermittent activity of its chemical thrusters, the slow oscillation in position, and the intensity of the blip on the screen. Finally he turned to Captain Hewes.

"What do you think, Frank?" he asked. "Tracking unit gone on the blink?"

As Sanborn spoke, George Foran, standing silent and superfluous beside the monitor, thought back over what he had learned about the tracking system used by the cargo carriers, a system employing a tiny pulse laser and a time-lapse deflection detector in each carrier. He knew in a general way how one sled followed another in twelve, long, flaring lines of eight each, forming a huge, hollow cone behind the ship, each sled tracking the one ahead and the twelve leaders tracking the *Pegasus*.

"No, I don't think it can be that, sir — at least not just that," Hewes responded. "There's something queer about that main voltage. I know it's being cut off by the directional sensors when the sled gets far enough off course — that's what it is supposed to do to allow the chemical thrusters to correct the deviation without having to work against actinic thrust. But then it should go back up to regular operating level, and it isn't doing that. It's getting back to only about fifty percent and hanging there for five seconds, then going off again for about ninety seconds. Lanny" — he turned to Lieutenant Munn, whose given name was Orlando — "has it been like this since the trouble started?"

"Yes sir, the intervals have not changed," responded the heavy-jawed junior officer.

"How about the guidance, sir? Suppose a couple of the steering heads were jammed?" Technician John Pryor interrupted in an obvious attempt to be helpful.

Again a spark of impatience glinted and was gone in Lieutenant Munn's black eyes as he thought, why doesn't that guy think before he pops off? But then he caught a flicker of amused interest in Colonel Sanborn's quick glance at Pryor and himself.

"It couldn't be, John," he explained patiently. "They aren't powerful enough to move the mass of a loaded sled around that quickly."

Pryor grinned, shamefaced. "Yes sir, I hadn't thought of that."

"But half a ring could!" ejaculated the Captain suddenly, thinking of the two concentric mounting rings on the rear of the sled, each ring closely studded with the big crystal emitters from which flashed the sled's propulsive energy. The steering heads were simply four pairs of emitters mounted on gimbals at ninety-degree intervals about the outer ring and connected to the guidance system — their combined output was enough to accomplish only very gradual control maneuvers without the use of precious chemical fuel. But twenty times that force, applied on one side of the mounting rings, would be enough to turn the sled quickly off course. And that, realized

Hewes, was just what would happen if one of the wiring harnesses failed, for the sled's drive was powered through two harnesses, each feeding half the circle of emitters on both inner and outer rings.

"We can soon find out," he said, half to himself, and moved abruptly over to the rear end of the master control console where he activated the remote command circuit that would operate on the same laser beam that was reading L-5's position in space. Shutting off the sled's actinic power, he signaled the chemical thrusters to take over primary propulsion, a function they were designed to perform as a back-up system.

"That's it!" cried the impulsive Pryor as the scanner image steadied and moved toward center screen.

Hewes turned to the Colonel. "The number one harness or its interface connector has to be the answer, sir."

"I think you're right, Captain. You will be wanting Larsen to send out a repair party, of course, but we'll continue normal acceleration except for the disabled sled. What is it carrying?"

"A hydroponic kit, I believe," replied Hewes with a questioning glance at Lieutenant Munn who nodded, then shot a you-better-be-right look at Pryor, who smiled confidently.

"Good. That's not immediately vital." Sanborn turned to go. "I'll be going right by Captain Larsen's office. I'll stop in and arrange for a repair detail to leave at once."

"Thank you, sir," acknowledged the Captain, then looked at Munn. "Shut down L-5. Let it coast and keep a beam on it. Better get working on an intercept course for the repair party. This is not a crash emergency so they will run a standard preflight check-out. Figure them to eject in thirty minutes."

# 9

I N THE RECREATION ROOM down on E-deck, Ray
Aseto sat motionless, impassive, his rough-hewn Mongo-
lian features expressionless save for a glint of amusement
in the opaque black eyes fixed on the man opposite, an
unhandsome redhead who studied the chessboard between them with well-founded suspicion. Harry Cohen
knew from experience that Aseto possessed a phenomenal
memory for the classic gambits of the game of kings,
along with a few wicked innovations of his own. Cohen,
too, was fascinated by the intricate labyrinths of attack
and defense. He took his beatings with good-natured
grumblings about the other's astounding luck, meanwhile
sharpening his own skill and memory toward the day
when he might have the luck on his side.

At first Aseto had thrown a game here and there, but the husky, brown-eyed Cohen had been shrewd enough to catch it and had finally refused to play again unless Aseto promised to stop.

Harry was about to castle when the speaker in the corner behind him clicked on and Captain Larsen's flat accents filled the room.

"Mister Aseto and Mister Foran to the B-deck ready room, on the double! Prepare to take out an auxiliary vehicle on a repair mission. Lieutenant Lin, Lieutenant Tandy: to my office at once!"

"Blast!" exploded Cohen. "Just when I was finally going to show you how to play this game, he has to call another rehearsal!"

"It is what your sand-eating ancestors used to call Kismet," replied Aseto smoothly, sliding out the door just ahead of the flying pawn and explosive reply hurled by his adversary. Cohen's Orthodox Jewish ancestors had fought bloody wars with their ethnic cousins of Muslim persuasion over stretches of sandy countryside, so the idea that those ancestors would use a Muslim term such as Kismet was sure to call forth a violent response. A flicker of a grin still twitched at Aseto's lips as he padded along, three decks higher, down the narrow passage toward the compartment where pressure suits, helmets, and gloves were kept. George Foran was already there, a look of eager excitement lighting his hazel eyes.

"Hello, kid," growled Ray with casual gruffness, masking a genuine fondness for the young man. "This your first outside job since we left?"

"Yeah," responded George, equally offhand, trying to give the impression that this was just one more boring duty to be performed. "I'll bet it's nothing but another drill — and just when Thomas had agreed to give me another half hour on the intercom." This referred to George's self-imposed task of stretching his knowledge of electronics to include the ship's communications system. He was constantly after Joel Lane and Ned Thomas, the communications technicians, to teach him principles and circuitry.

But the complaint carried little conviction. His eyes glowed with anticipation.

"Tough luck," agreed Aseto, straight-faced, as he worked one stocking-clad foot into a leg of his pressure suit. The tough, flexible material was compounded of glass fiber and synthetic filament to give some ease of movement while affording maximum resistance to pressure loss and perforation. The suit was also designed to protect against harmful radiations, all the way from low-frequency infrared waves up through ultraviolet, X-ray and gamma-ray frequencies and beyond to the incredibly tiny wavelengths of energy at which are found electrons, positrons, cosmic wavicles, and antiprotons.

"You know, kid," Ray went on, "this might not be just

[ 6 5 ]

another dry run. The Captain sounded tougher than usual, and he called in Tandy, who finished his watch half an hour ago. I got an idea this is for real."

Both men were standing now, helping each other with the last fitting and fastening of their suits, in a routine that was already second nature. Finished, they picked up helmets and gloves and left the room.

The launch and recovery compartment occupied one third of B-deck and was an airtight section, which meant that its doors were air locks of cylindrical design, through which two men passed at a time. Aseto and Foran, entering through the rear door, made their way quickly down the row of teardrop-shaped auxiliary craft, the four A-Cs, which were ranged along the left side of the compartment. Each of their pointed sterns terminated in a stubby rocket nozzle protruding backward from the center of a small power ring. Both chemical and actinic thrust capability were available to give the craft the range and speed to meet any likely situation. Each A-C would accommodate three people, two of whom made up a basic work party while the third functioned as pilot, communications man, safety man, or whatever else might be required.

Arriving beside the A-C nearest the launching cage, George swung open the door, put his helmet on one of the seats, and took up the check-off sheet he and Aseto would sign, declaring the flight readiness of the small craft. Item by item they worked their way through the list, beginning with the focused field reactor that powered the electric and electronic systems which ran or monitored virtually every function of the craft and its occupants. Then there were the systems themselves to be activated: guidance, communications, automatic and manual control, life-support, the small computer whose logic and memory ran or backed up the systems. There were tanks of fuel and oxidizer for the rocket and attitude jets, tanks of oxygen for the pressure suits, a tank of compressed air for the craft itself, a tank of drinking water, and a sanitary tank. There were dehydrated foods, first-aid supplies, spare parts, tools, safety line, backpack thrusters, one spare suit. It seemed impossible that the little craft could contain all the items they checked off and still provide room for three men, but somehow it did. Ten minutes saw them through the list of preliminaries to launching.

The launching mechanism was a catapult, as simplified as skill and ingenuity could make it, like everything else in and about the ship. Accounting for but nine pounds of design weight, it included a pressure tank hooked up to the launch chamber evacuating pump, a solenoid valve, a cylinder, piston, and rod that was shaped to engage a peg on the A-Cs' launching cradles. This simple toy sufficed to shove out into space two thousand pounds of men, ship, and equipment because they weighed only one hundred pounds in the fifty milligee "gravity" induced by the ship's soft acceleration.

"Check the peg, kid," grunted Aseto. He had signed the check-off sheet and clipped it to the launch officer's panel while Foran was releasing the locking bar under the leading A-C and sliding it forward into the launching chamber, the back of which would be swung to and locked and most of the air pumped out of the chamber before the big, circular port could be retracted and slid open for the actual launch.

"Okay, boss," George grinned and stooped to see that the impeller engaged the launching peg as Aseto put the catapult in place. "Right in the bucket, boss," he added, holding up a closed thumb and forefinger.

At that moment the door in the rear of the L and R compartment opened, and Lieutenant Lin, clad in a pressure suit and carrying helmet and gloves, strode in as precisely as one can stride in a one-twentieth gravity environment, where a firm step will boost a person two feet in the air. With him was Captain Larsen, thick-set and abrupt of speech and manner but constrained to move with the same gentle deliberation as everyone else, by the lack of weight. The Captain was in charge of construction and maintenance for the expedition and chief engineer of the *Pegasus*.

Again the air-lock door swung open to admit the muscular figure of Ed Mayer who, with Aseto, Cohen, and Foran, constituted the noncommissioned roster of Larsen's plant and propulsion section. Like a big panther he flatfooted along behind the others, past bays, bins, and racks containing spare rocket nozzles, reactor casings, interrupter rods, gyro kits, Angstrom filters, and hundreds of other parts and tools that might be needed instantly if original equipment failed. A stranger, watching all the cargo sleds out there behind them, might have thought that there were not enough replacement parts on hand, not knowing that there were plenty more in two of the nearest sleds. Those familiar with the expedition's logistical struggles were acutely aware that only the most selective use of every cubic foot of space inside *Pegasus* and her herd of metallic followers had made the journey possible from the two points of functional efficiency and safety.

Lin stopped long enough to say something to Mayer who turned and picked up a long package from one of the bins before continuing toward the waiting A-C One, where he handed it to Aseto. When the latter saw it was a wiring harness, he gave Foran a brief I-told-you-so smile.

The two officers glanced down the check-off list, then entered the launch chamber where Aseto reported the little craft ready to go.

"Good," replied Lin, his clipped Oxford accents contrasting oddly with the straight black hair, black eyes, and flat profile bequeathed him by his Cantonese ancestors.

"We shall be going quite a distance. One of the cargo carriers has developed propulsion trouble."

"Sorry to interrupt your off-duty time, Mister Aseto," said Captain Larsen, "but it can't be helped. I'm sure Mister Cohen's lesson can wait," he added dryly.

"Yes, sir," grinned Aseto, surprised at Larsen's familiarity with the one-sided character of his contests with Cohen.

"Now," Larsen backed out of the chamber, "if you're ready, gentlemen, we want to get that sled back in running order just as soon as possible, so let's get on with it."

There was no sarcasm in the Captain's tone. If anything, quite the opposite; he was too concerned with having anything he undertook done right, and right away, to waste time on pettiness. The men in his command had sensed this early in the job of assembling and equipping the *Pegasus,* when it became clear that he was always brief to the point of curtness but civil and quite prepared to take over any job he criticized. He could usually do it better and faster, at the same time providing a lucid explanation.

Into the A-C went Foran, Lin, and Aseto, the Lieutenant at the controls. As they adjusted their seat harnesses, the rear door of the launch and recovery compartment slid into place and a thin whine commenced as the air in the chamber was sucked back into the main compartment. Sealing the repair craft's hatch, they donned helmets and gloves, tested suit pressures and helmet radios. Once safely launched, they would remove the cumbersome headgear and gloves until needed for the outside work.

Up ahead an orange light came on above the big circular port, indicating that the residual air in the chamber was being vented outward. Thirty seconds later the port retracted and slid aside. Beyond glowed the starlit darkness of space.

"A-C One to Bridge." Lin spoke into his throat mike, his precise voice ringing in the ears of his fellow passengers and sounding tinnily over the intercom in the L and R compartment behind them, where Larsen and Mayer watched closely through the view plates. "Requesting permission to launch. Come in, please."

"Bridge to A-C One — you may launch when ready," came Lieutenant Munn's deeper voice. "Switch to remote control at a thousand yards. We will fly you to your target. Acknowledge."

"Remote control at a thousand yards," repeated Lin. "Safety off." He flicked a switch on the panel before him and a locking pin beneath the craft retracted with an audible clink, while at the same instant a red light winked on above the launch switch toggle to warn that the launch circuit was live. With the systems monitor showing a "go," Lin threw the switch.

A thud — a brief shove — then darkness except for

the dim cockpit and instrument lights and the distant stars.

On the Bridge a chronometer, activated by photocell relay, began to keep track of the small ship's elapsed mission time, while two laser tracking units, mounted on the outer hull in a way that gave one or the other a view of its target at all times, began feeding course and distance data to the computer channel that would monitor and control the flight. The distance information was derived by time-lapse measurement, a technique used in celestial physics and astrogation for determining the distance of an object by bouncing a laser or radar beam off of it and picking up the "echo," or return reflection.

In the L and R compartment, A-C Two was moved up into standby position as quickly as the port could be closed and the ambient pressure of nine and a half pounds per square inch restored in the chamber. Until A-C One returned, it would stay there, with Mayer and one of the ship's two medics also on standby, ready to go on a minute's notice. This was standard procedure whenever a repair craft left the ship, even for the routine outer-hull inspections that were made every other day.

# 10

A PRECARIOUS, twisting vertigo assailed Lieutenant Henry Lin at the moment A-C One thrust out of the launching port into the abyss. The same thing had happened on the occasion of his first deep-space launch when for a frightening instant he had thought he was going to have to ask his copilot to take over. But then the unpleasant sensation had passed, and he had been all right. So now he clenched his jaws and held himself rigid to avoid betraying his feelings to the others, while a detached corner of his mind wondered whether either of his companions were similarly troubled. In a moment the dizziness subsided.

Waiting for the A-C to drift far enough from the ship's side to use the rocket engine without scorching the

*Pegasus,* Henry's mind toyed with the idea of questioning the others about their sensations at the moment of launching, but he knew it would be useless. Foran was too young and self-conscious to admit any weakness he could hide, while Aseto was a stubborn half-breed (Lin felt a twinge of guilt at his own unconscious snobbery), a stubborn half-breed whose Ainu grandfather had emigrated from Hokkaido to Pearl Harbor and married an Oahu girl. Aseto would never be anything but dutiful and impassively polite to Henry, whose own Cantonese ancestry enabled him to understand the innate nature of this reserve.

Now far enough from the big ship, Lin squeezed off a short burst of light thrust to hasten their progress toward the thousand-yard mark. The rocket behind them coughed, rasped briefly, and fell silent, coinciding with the gentle pressure of padded seats against their backs.

During this interval George Foran, whose in-flight duties as occupant of the left-hand seat would come later, was again gazing in spellbound fascination at the eternal wonder of the visible universe seen without an obscuring blanket of atmosphere. Beyond the clear plexite port, endless depths met his eager eyes. Automatically he reached up and removed his helmet, prompted by the fact that the others were doing the same now that the launching was safely accomplished.

"Suit overheating, George?" asked Aseto. "You're sweating."

"Yeah. Must be," replied Foran, running a surprised hand across his wet forehead. He turned back the thermal control. "That ought to do it."

"Coming up on a thousand yards."

It was Lieutenant Munn's voice, from the cockpit speaker. At the same time the video screen quivered to life and the Lieutenant looked out at them. This dual medium of communication was known as LETWAVE, for Light Energized Two Way Audio-Visual Exchange. It operated through modulation of the laser-tracking beams, thus eliminating the need for a separate system.

"You may switch to remote control," directed Munn. "We have you locked in. We shall be using one-gee acceleration —" here Munn smiled, "— so sit back and enjoy the ride; it will be a relief from floating around like a feather in *Pegasus*. Stand by for attitude change to 0-270-335 and acceleration." Lin acknowledged the instructions and gave the order to prepare for acceleration.

Drawing his harness straps tight, Foran glanced briefly at the view screen, then turned back almost as if mesmerized, to stare out the port, feeling as he did so a vague tightness behind his eyes. With an impatient blink, he shut his mind to it; no headache was going to spoil this priceless experience.

Just then the attitude jets crackled faintly and the A-C tilted, sending a streaming river of stars flowing diagonally across the porthole. A tiny, bright lancet of pain jabbed and was gone in George's head, succeeded by an overwhelming, clammy sense of disaster that clutched at him without warning or apparent reason. Panicky, he ran his eyes over the instrument panel but could find nothing amiss there. A sidelong glance at the others was no more helpful; they looked unperturbed.

Clamping a twitching lower lip between his teeth and staring straight ahead, George fought to control himself. Nothing like this had happened to him during his tour of duty in Earth orbit or during construction of the spaceship and his training in the operation of these auxiliary craft.

"Come on!" he admonished himself silently, "Cut it out. If there was anything wrong it would show on the board — and it doesn't."

At that moment the rocket behind them whumped to life and took up a dull rumble, shoving them all back in their seats with the equivalent of earthside weight. Coincidentally George's inexplicable apprehension faded, his muscles relaxed, and he felt all right again. Relieved but scared, he searched his mind for an explanation, without success. It was almost as if he had been thrust for a terrifying moment into a strange, distorted dimension. There was something else, too, something to do with the massive, reassuring bulk of Earth, no longer massive or reassuring, no longer nearby to be sensed if not always seen — his brain seemed unwilling to pursue the implications of this line of thought.

Foran's uneasy speculations were interrupted by Lin's voice.

"I expect you would like to know what this is all about," he said, looking from one to the other.

Aseto's politely attentive manner and automatic "Yes, sir," were about what Lin expected, but the absence of interest in the strangely set look Foran turned on him was a surprise, for the young technician's usual animated eagerness was missing. Lin hesitated an instant, then went on.

"One of the cargo sleds has developed engine trouble," he explained. "L-5, in the nine o'clock wing. Navigation says it acts like a wiring harness has quit, leaving the sled with a lopsided thrust."

At the Lieutenant's words, Ray Aseto pictured their destination, far out along one of the files of carriers radiating diagonally backward and outward behind the *Pegasus*. The giant truncated cone enclosed a thousand cubic miles within the twelve files of eight sleds, each positioned so that no sled's line of flight was closer than two thousand yards to that of another, while the nearest were four thousand yards from the ship.

The sleds were equipped, Ray knew, with laser tracking systems that kept them on station. To avoid generating a snap-the-whip effect, there was a time delay factor in the guidance program that ignored small, erratic changes of course involved in keeping station, as well as the periodic waves of corkscrewing that passed through the fleet in regular, slow sweeps. These latter gyrations were damped out by each carrier's stabilizer without any trouble, but no one seemed to know what caused them. In the present situation Ray assumed, correctly, that the disabled carrier had been shut down and the one behind it commanded to ignore the double interval and track on the one next ahead.

"Deceleration will begin in fifteen seconds, A-C One," grated the speaker as Lieutenant Munn's features slid into view on the screen. "Attitude reversal beginning now."

Even as he spoke the roar of the rocket died away, and they hung weightless in their harnesses for a split second. Then the little ship spun on its vertical axis a half circle, and the muted roar recommenced. The pressure of contour seats against their backs, after the abrupt half-turn, made it seem that they were hurrying back over the route they had just followed. There were no references outside to show that they were scooting along backward, the rocket now working to kill off the 1900-

feet-a-second speed they had attained after 58 seconds of acceleration. At the same level of thrust, a nearly equal time of deceleration would be needed to bring them to a stop near the L-5 sled, at which point Lin would take manual control.

# 11

THE DISTANT *Pegasus* hung centered in their field of vision, the ship itself invisible behind the spectacular green-white eye of brilliance that marked its multiple thrust beam some ten miles away. This was the first opportunity for each of them to see his ship underway, at a distance that made it safe to look at the blinding glare. Their viewing angle blended the quivering thrust cones of actinic energy from its thirty-three power rings into a single, vibrant, square-cut emerald of frozen radiance, at which they gazed in momentary, spellbound silence.

Finally George Foran spoke, in an awed tone. "It's really — beautiful, isn't it?" He stole a glance at the others, the gusty alarm of a moment ago temporarily forgotten.

"Very impressive," agreed Lin, trying hard to keep any trace of defensive condescension out of his voice. The sharp awareness of his own wordless emotional response to the beautiful sight annoyed the logical, pragmatic part of his mind and embarrassed him. He smiled briefly at Foran but couldn't bring himself to turn and look for agreement in Aseto's black eyes lest he find instead ridicule for one who entertained such soft, womanish sentiments. Setting his lips, he busied himself with an intent study of the instrument panel.

Ray Aseto was thinking, oddly enough, of his paternal grandfather whom he had seen on only two occasions, as a child, when the formidable, white-haired old man had appeared briefly from some mysterious, distant place to visit and bless his wandering third son and family on their San Fernando Valley truck farm. With his high cheekbones, reddish complexion, dark eyes and bold nose, the old man might have passed as a Western Indian and may well have shared a common Mongol ancestry with them in that far-off time when the nomads of the Siberian steppes migrated east and south in search of more hospitable living conditions. Ray carried an indelible impression of the proud, patriarchal figure and of the way his own parents had accepted without question the elder man's opinions and judgments. Somewhere, too, Ray still had the only letter his grandfather had ever written him, shortly after his second visit, during which time young Ray and he had become fast friends. Two sentences of the short letter Ray had never forgotten: "Know that to live is to give — love, to those close to you; friendship, to those who will honor it; praise, to those who deserve it; respect, to those who merit it. Don't be ashamed to admire a brave man, a lovely woman, a beautiful thing." The wisdom of the old man's words had become more apparent to Ray as he grew old enough to see so many people discontented and unhappy because they sought only to take from life.

Now he found himself hoping against all reason that his grandfather's spirit could somehow be aware of the spine-tingling beauty of this unique moment in which the embodiment of mankind's eternal quest rode like a bright new star in the timeless, dim reaches of space. Glad that George had mustered the courage to comment, he felt a surge of impatient scorn for the Lieutenant's patronizing tone and choice of words. When they got back to the ship, he resolved, he would share something of his own pleasure with the young man.

Behind them the rocket droned steadily, wavering a little from time to time as it responded to the directional impulses reaching its gimbaled mount from the *Pegasus's* computer. A little side trip like this was simplicity itself back on Earth where fuel was plentiful and gravity provided the friction needed to start, stop, and turn. Out here, with fuel precious and gravity virtually nonexistent, they were dependent on the computer's magic to pilot the repair craft along a flat curve that would place it alongside the disabled carrier with the smallest expenditure of fuel. It is difficult to conceive the number and kind of factors that enter into such a calculation, for man's senses are neither designed nor conditioned to respond to very big or very little stimuli, especially those without a perceptible basis for comparison. As Colonel Benjamin Marcus, the expedition's brilliant young astrophysical chief, had said, man is such an inefficient scientific instrument that he would be thrown out of any responsible laboratory if the machines could take care of themselves.

Lin, looking at the instrument array, was thinking of some of these things as he waited for the rocket to cease: the *Pegasus* and cargo carriers accelerating at a foot and a half a second — the L-5 that had stopped accelerating and was coasting at whatever velocity it had attained when its power ws cut — A-C One, which had ceased to share the convoy's acceleration when it was launched, had acquired a sideways momentum from the catapult and its own rocket, and was growing steadily lighter as it expended fuel. He could visualize the streams of data flowing through the computer's input and being shunted to their destinations like streams of traffic entering a metropolis and dispersing to their various goals, each bit of information helping to construct and modify the output that guided the repair craft to its goal.

"Helmets and gloves, gentlemen," he said. "We shall be arriving directly. Mister Foran, you will stand by the controls while Mister Aseto and I make an inspection."

Foran, relieved that he would not be compelled to clamber out into empty space just yet, nevertheless felt vaguely uneasy as he slipped the big helmet over his head. Annoyed, he thrust the feeling aside with a wordless admonition to his queasy spirits to snap out of it. He knew, though, that when he did have to leave the auxiliary craft, it was going to take an effort of will.

The muffled roar and vibration behind them died out, and they hung weightless. From the view screen, Lieutenant Munn looked at them and said, "That does it, Lieutenant. We are turning you one hundred and eighty degrees in yaw axis. You will find the L-5 approximately fifty yards ahead, at rest with respect to your craft. Assume manual control and effect rendezvous. We shall stand by for your report of contact."

The A-C One swiveled and steadied in response to the thrust of attitude jets, and its three occupants peered ahead as Lin flicked on a brilliant strobe light.

There, glinting against the dark backdrop, hung the lifeless sled, several times the size of their small ship. Actually it was tumbling slowly end over end, and they blinked at the sharp stab of sunlight reflecting momentarily from its wide, slightly convex front surface.

"Secure helmets. Prepare for blowdown," instructed Lin, closing his own faceplate and switching on his suit tank of oxygen. Plain oxygen was used in the pressure suits rather than the nitrogen-oxygen mix found aboard ship because the high-energy output required to work in a weightless environment was more easily sustained in an oxygen atmosphere.

"Blow down to four pounds," ordered Lin, and the three men went to work on the several steps involved in lowering cabin pressure. Foran shut down the air filtering, scrubbing, and recirculating system while Aseto turned off the regular and emergency automatic pressure supplies and put one hand on the manual emergency pressure valve.

"Pressure system off. Standing by manual," he reported.

"Environment off," added Foran.

Lin opened the cockpit exhaust valve, and they watched the gauge needle hang motionless at nine and a half pounds for a long moment, then slip grudgingly down the scale to just under four pounds, at which point Lin closed the valve and the needle edged back up fractionally to rest on the four-pound mark. Each of them rechecked his suit for pressure integrity, after which Lin reopened the valve, allowing the last of the air to whistle out. One more suit check and Lin, flipping the navigation control switch to manual, eased the A-C into within twenty yards of the carrier, where he stopped it and turned to Foran.

"Aseto and I will get out here. I shall board the carrier and halt that spin with the manual controls in the service panel. If the carrier makes any move other than to slow down the spin, you get this craft out of range at once and keep it there. Aseto," he turned to the white-suited figure on his right, "you stay clear until I give you the word. Got it?"

Both indicated they had it.

"Mister Aseto, open your hatch and stand by to put on a backpack and safety line."

Following a routine established through experimentation and perfected by many rehearsals, Aseto slid the hatch open and pulled himself part way through, stopping in a half crouch with his back to the others. Lin, bracing both legs between the seats, reached out and slipped a backpack harness over the other's head, then tightened shoulder and thigh clips and control belt.

"All right," he said, hooking a coiled safety line to Aseto's belt, "go ahead."

Aseto relaxed his grip on the hatch coaming, straightened his legs, and floated smoothly out of the A-C, provoking a stabilizing puff of vapor from the opposite attitude jets.

Using the additional room provided by Aseto's departure, Lin donned his own gear and eased out, one hand on the stubby control knob of the backpack thrusters.

A few yards away, the bulky figure of Aseto hung like an inflated white mannequin, face toward the A-C but horizontally, as if lying on an invisible bed. Beneath him the L-5 rolled ponderously, sunlight glaring from its face and flat rear end at slow intervals. The sun itself was below and behind Lin's position at the moment. He could change that, of course, by using his thrusters and have the sun above him, but then the A-C would be upside down right in front of him. He was reminded of part of a talk Captain Finberg had given at one of the preflight lectures.

"If your senses are bothered by a lack of orientation references, bear in mind that our solar system is heliocentric, as the name implies. No matter where you are in the system or what your attitude with relation to any other body may be, a line from you to the sun is, for that point, straight up."

The old, annoying feeling of wordless wonder gripped Lin — annoying because he disliked feeling inadequate, even to so awesome a task as describing satisfactorily the scope and beauty of the visible universe. Dominating the scene, of course, was the sun, a shrunken, intensely white ball, too brilliant to regard without the protection of his glare visor. Turning away, he sought out his own binary

Earth-Moon, curious to see whether he could distinguish the one from the other at a fifty-odd-million-mile range. The two were one, he found, a bright blue-white star over his left shoulder, not much bigger than the red one to his right, toward which they were heading, and definitely smaller looking than the globe of Venus, which they would pass close by.

But there were more concrete matters demanding his attention.

"I am going to land on the sled now and stop its rotation," he said into his throat mike. "Aseto, you stay clear until I call you aboard."

Acknowledging the order, Ray watched the other propel himself in a slow arc to land in the center of L-5's flat rear end, surrounded by the two fencelike, concentric rings of its emitters. The rolling sled carried Lin's crouching figure out of sight for a minute, and when he reappeared, Ray saw that he had the hinged cover of the safety panel open. This mandatory first step in all cargo-carrier work served the dual purpose of cutting off the power and of making accessible the manual controls operating the chemical fuel attitude jets. The crouching white-clad figure clung to the cover plate with one hand and reached down into the square hole beneath it with the other. A second later long streamers of white vapor shot out from four points equally spaced around the sled's rim, their force directed counter to the carrier's spin. In little more than a minute the jets, swiveling back and forth under Lin's guiding hand, brought the spin to a halt, or as nearly so as mattered for their purposes. Now the sun illuminated the rear deck.

Lieutenant Lin straightened up carefully on his knees, keeping a grip on the panel so he wouldn't float off the deck, and lifted a beckoning arm toward the waiting Aseto.

"All right, come aboard," he said briskly. Nucleonics and nuclear power plants were his special discipline, and the subconscious awareness of his complete competence lent vigor and authority to his usually detached manner. Looking about, he located A-C One's bright strobe light and glittering small shape off to one side, slightly above the sled's rim.

"Mister Foran, report us aboard the cargo carrier and commencing examination of the propulsion unit," instructed Lin via his helmet radio. "Tell them we will report on the damage as soon as possible. Then close in to twenty feet and stand by. Mister Aseto, when Foran gets here, have him break out replacement fuel and oxidant flasks for you to put into the carrier's propellant system. The ones aboard show a fifteen percent depletion, over half the amount allowed for in-transit maneuvers. We'll take no chance of running short at the other end."

The "other end" was the landing operation on Mars, during which time the sleds' chemical thrusters would be called upon to expend three-quarters of their starting load of propellant in generating and maintaining a rapid spin of the saucerlike carriers and in braking and cooling functions.

Lin turned his attention now to the sled's wiring harnesses. The two harnesses started as thick cables leading from outlets in the deck, each surrounded by a shallow metal collar. Running around the deck in a semicircle between the two power rings, each cable became progressively thinner as the slender leads to the individual laser pumps branched off from it. Spotting one of the outlets, Lin shoved himself gently toward it, grasping a ring strut to check his momentum. As he reached a point where he could see down into the collar, he stared in amazement. The inside of the cuplike fixture was a mess of black, charred insulation, and the fiber wheel that should have girdled the cable to center it in the metal collar was just not there. Looking closer, he perceived that the cable itself was completely gone, burnt off for a space of about two inches just above its plug-in fitting. The severed end dangled level with the top of the collar.

# 12

GEORGE FORAN, searching out the spaceship's thrust cone as he prepared to deliver the Lieutenant's message, was surprised to see how it had dwindled since his last look. At first he couldn't even locate it, as he pivoted the repair craft to face what he thought was the proper direction. A flare of apprehension tightened his stomach muscles. Then he spotted it, a glittering fleck off to his left, edging up on a steep slant into a fathomless, dim immensity spangled with similar flecks. The spaceship's unexpected position and course must have offended his senses in some obscure way, for again a sharp twinge of pain jabbed in his head and was gone. Hurriedly he called the Bridge and delivered Lin's message, then swung the craft about to move in on the cargo sled as instructed.

[ 9 1 ]

Part way around, the gleaming star that was his home planet swam, bright and beckoning, across the open hatch to his right, and all at once he was seized by an unreasoning urge to jam the little ship's rocket throttle wide open, cut in the actinic drive, and head for home!

"What the devil's the matter with me?" he thought, genuinely frightened now as he fought down the insane impulse. Cautiously he guided the auxiliary craft in toward the L-5. "Maybe I'd better tell Lieutenant Lin there's something wrong with me before it gets any worse."

The impulse to head for Earth had left him as suddenly as it had struck, but his undershirt was stuck to his back and a slight tremor made his hand quiver on the control stick as he moved it to halt the repair craft near the rim of the big sled. Waiting there for Aseto to come over for the replacement flasks of fuel and oxidant, he tried to make up his mind about what he should do. The Lieutenant, he was sure, would suspend the repair job and rush him back to the ship if he told him. Somehow that thought, with the whole crew knowing that he'd failed his first real test, was more than he could stand. He resolved to stick it out, to do what was required of him, and then to see Doc Finberg as soon as they got back.

By the time Aseto came drifting over for the fuel cylinders, Foran had them out and waiting.

Over on the back of the cargo carrier, Lieutenant Lin

let go of the burnt end of the wiring harness and spoke into his throat mike.

"Mister Aseto, bring back the short aligning rod when you come. Mister Foran, tell the ship that L-5's number-one wiring harness is burnt off just outside the coupling, apparently fused by a short circuit. Then get out the spare harness we brought and stand by to bring it over when I get through here and relieve you. If navigation wants an estimated time to complete repairs, tell them fifteen minutes."

From where he knelt on the sled's rear deck, Lin could see Foran's helmeted head turn as he acknowledged the order and gave the message to the *Pegasus*. Waiting for Aseto to return with the slender, pointed rod he was going to use to clean out the fitting, he saw that the sled's tiny residual momentum had rolled it to where the sunlight was about to be cut off, so he slid over to the square recess in the deck and reached in for the manual control handle. Noting that the diminutive A-C would be uncomfortably close to the sweep of the sled's rim, he backed the larger craft away a few feet before completing the maneuver.

"All right," he said to Aseto, hovering between the two craft, "come ahead." Keeping a firm grip on the cover plate, he checked the flask-burdened technician's momentum, took the aligning rod, and eased himself back to the power outlet.

The blackened area within the outlet collar and the black gobs of burned insulation clinging to it had absorbed enough direct infrared radiation from the sun's rays to soften the tarry deposits to an extent that allowed Lin to scrape them off the metal with the flattened end of the rod. For want of a better place to put the sticky mess, he scraped it off against the outside of the collar itself and was surprised to see how quickly, in the absence of effective gravity and atmospheric pressure, the gluey substance softened and spread on the hot metal. He kept expecting it to slide down onto the carrier's deck until its failure to do so reminded him that there was nothing to make it fall down. With the last of the deposits cleaned out Lin took hold of the removable upper part of the interface connector, or plug, that had formerly been part of the wiring harness and applied a pushing, twisting force to unlock it, half expecting to find it fused and immovable. To his relief, the plug turned and pulled out of its fixture quite normally, exposing the female half of the bayonet connector, still retaining the spring in place and looking as bright as new.

"Well," he thought, "it looks all right. Only way to be sure is to put on the new harness and try it."

Improvised cleaning rod and damaged plug in hand, he straightened slowly, allowing the momentum of the act to carry him clear of the sled's deck. As he checked his drift with the backpack, he saw that Aseto was nearly finished installing the second fuel cylinder, which meant he would be free to help Foran put the new harness on. Another nudge with the thruster sent him floating leisurely toward the A-C.

"Mister Foran, get out your backpack, and I'll help you into it," Lin called. "Then you may begin disconnecting the number-one harness leads. Here," he added as he reached the open hatch, "put both of these in a locker." He held out the damaged plug and the rod. "Oh, take a wiper along to clean out the connector fitting and collar, and be certain not to get any dirt into the plug. Wipe the outside of the collar last so you can get a good-sized gob of burnt insulation for us to analyze. Got it?" he added as the other hesitated.

"Yes sir," responded Foran almost roughly, taking the rod and plug from Lin's outstretched hand and stowing them away with what seemed unnecessary deliberation.

Lin, not sure the roughness and deliberation weren't of his own imagining, contented himself with a brief, "Make it as quick as you can. Fuel is precious."

"Yes sir, I know."

The young technician's tone this time was thin but respectful, and he moved a bit faster as he hooked a coiled safety line and a wiping rag to his work belt, then donned a backpack with Lin's assistance. Poised on the edge of the hatch, he again hesitated, clinging to the coaming.

"Shall I take the new harness, sir?" he asked, in the same thin, carefully articulated voice as before.

"No. Aseto is through; he can bring it. You concentrate on getting the old one off and the fixture clean."

"All right, sir."

Still gripping the hatch rim firmly, Foran slowly picked one foot, then the other, off the sill and pushed himself clumsily toward a spot somewhere above the cargo carrier's deck.

Clambering into the little repair ship, Lieutenant Lin shed his backpack and slid over into the pilot's seat, wondering why the other's awkward method of departure looked familiar. Then he recalled that it was one of the break-in routines in weightless maneuvering, designed to help trainees realize that, without gravity, the concepts of "stand up" and "fall down" had no reality. Strange he should still do that, thought Lin.

# 13

FOR GEORGE FORAN the last few minutes had taken on more and more the quality of a nightmare. He had just begun to regain control of his jumpy nerves when the bulky, white-clad figure of the Lieutenant loomed up by the open hatch, and George was shocked to realize that he had been neglecting his primary responsibility as anchor man of the work party — that of watching the two outside constantly, holding himself alert to go instantly to the help of either or both. This duty had absolute first claim on the inboard man's attention because only instant response by him offered any hope of life to the victim of a blowout or torn suit. The shock of knowing that one — or both — of his companions might have died while he sat there fighting his private battle left

Foran's nerves tighter than ever. He had to force his acknowledgment of Lin's orders through tightly constricted throat muscles, and his head swam as he bent to stow the damaged harness connection and aligning rod handed him by the Lieutenant, causing him to move with unusual slowness. Out of the corner of his eye he saw Lin's puzzled look, and he knew the latter's admonition to hurry up was deserved, yet a hot little flicker of irritation flared in the back of his mind. Somehow he managed a civil response and a more normal pace as he assembled the needed items and squirmed into a backpack. The dizziness seemed to grow less important as he forced himself to keep moving, though it was no less present and a low thrumming had started inside his head. Poised on the rim of the hatch, he all but gave up as the growing, surflike roar that now filled his skull seemed to be scattering his thoughts into elusive fragments. With a desperate effort of will he forced the tumult aside long enough to recall the nature of his errand and to wonder why he did not have the new harness in his hands. Shaping each word with painful care, he asked the waiting Lin, hanging grimly on each word of the reply to seize its meaning before it should be lost in the surging din within him. Somehow he must get aboard the carrier, wipe out the empty fixture, and disconnect the broken harness.

As he squinted to make out the cargo sled's deck, his eyesight seemed to be traveling down a long, gray tunnel, at the end of which was his goal, shrunken and glittering painfully in the reflected sunlight. Confused, panicky, aware that something was very wrong, yet driven on by the memory of a resolve whose details were lost, he straightened his legs one at a time and shoved convulsively outward. The effort triggered a bright, stabbing pain behind his eyeballs and the roaring in his head swelled into a great avalanche of sound that swept away everything — sight, feeling, even at last the sound itself, in an all-engulfing wave of darkness.

George opened his eyes and looked about in bewilderment. What was he doing out here in empty space, fully suited and helmeted, drifting above a lifeless cargo sled on the rear end of which crouched an astronaut holding an orange fuel cylinder under one arm and just picking up a green oxidant cylinder? He could remember only that he, Aseto, and Lieutenant Lin had ejected from *Pegasus* in an A-C, only three or four seconds ago, their destination unspecified but involving a new wiring harness. Looking closer, he saw that the sled's number-one harness, apparently intact throughout its two parallel half circles of laser pump connections, was loose from its deck plug, which showed the black streaking of an electrical burn.

At that moment his head set clicked on.

"OK George, go to it!" said Aseto's voice.

At the same time, the figure below, too big to be Lin, pushed carefully off the sled toward the nearby A-C, a cylinder clutched under either arm. Foran barely kept himself from calling after the departing figure to find out what he was supposed to do, but he knew that anything he said to Aseto would be heard by Lin, and something made him refrain. The answer was almost a certainty anyhow, for there he was, and there was the broken harness to be removed. Still, he could feel the cold sweat start as he eased down and began to disconnect the harness. The same queer feeling that had kept him from speaking out made his scalp prickle at the thought that he might be doing something other than what was expected of him.

"I'll be back with the new one in a minute, kid," called Aseto as he arrived at the open hatch of the repair craft. "Make sure that fixture's wiped out good and clean."

Foran's muscles relaxed at this confirmation of his choice of activity, and he made no response to the other's perfunctory admonition. Very much aware, in some undefined way, that all was not as it should be within him, he knew that any serious criticism or reprimand would destroy his precarious self-control. He must keep himself tightly aloof until he could get back to the security of his quarters aboard the *Pegasus,* where he could be alone and try to penetrate the dark knot of fear

that blotted out all recollection of the immediate past.
Beneath this conscious awareness and purpose there
lurked another shadowy intuition that something un-
healthy had had its way with him during the forgotten
interval, something that he must uncover and cleanse
himself of quickly or be destroyed.

Disconnecting the last lead, he turned to the smudged
deck outlet, thinking of Aseto's last words. Then he
stopped dead, apprehension again tightening his muscles.
He had no recollection of even leaving the A-C, let alone
bringing along a cloth to wipe out the fixture! Half afraid,
he felt at his belt, breathing a sigh of relief when his
gloved hand encountered the wiper. Hurriedly he set to
work removing the dark smudges from the fixture, even
as Aseto landed behind him and began attaching the
new harness.

"L-5 ready to test when you are," Lin reported to the
*Pegasus* some ten minutes later. "New harness and fresh
fuel tanks installed. If you're set to monitor, I'll run a
test, then you can bring us in if it checks out all right."

"Go ahead with the test, Lieutenant; we're ready,"
came Munn's reply, accompanied by an oddly relieved
look.

During the testing and the subsequent return to the
*Pegasus,* George Foran sat silent and rigid except when
he reached over to turn on the environment controls that
were his part of the repressurizing operation. Meanwhile

he tried again and again to force his way into the walled-off compartment of his mind in which the events of the trip to the cargo carrier must be recorded. But it was as if the recording tape had been erased from a point just after they left the ship to the instant when he opened his eyes and beheld the L-5 below. He tried imagining what must have taken place and attempting to remember corresponding scenes — to no avail. Silently he bemoaned the fate that had made him a member of the repair party, more and more convinced that there was a vital link between something that had taken place in that blacked-out bit of his life and the nameless fear that lurked just beneath the surface of his mind.

Finally, as they floated in toward the *Pegasus,* George realized that it was no go. Between the strain of keeping up an outward composure and concentrating inwardly on the vain attempt at recollection, his head throbbed painfully and his stomach was sore from the pressure of taut muscles. Forcing himself to act and speak as though nothing were wrong, he went methodically through the check-out routine, returned his pressure suit to the locker, and then hurried to his quarters.

# 14

LIEUTENANT LIN, unaware of the building tumult in the mind of his younger crew member, was climbing out of his pressure suit in the launch and recovery compartment of the *Pegasus,* assisted by his fellow junior officer in the plant and propulsion section, Lieutenant Tandy. As they waited for the technicians to complete the postflight check of the A-C One, Lin described what he had found wrong with the cargo carrier.

"It must have been a short, Amos. There was a quarter-inch hole melted right through the metal collar that stands up around the deck plug, and the inside of the collar and fitting was covered with black, charred insulation — that stuff there." Lin pointed to the soiled wiping cloth. "But the thing is impossible! There's a two-inch gap between the cable and the metal housing, and that's two inches of high vacuum. Besides, the cable is shielded." Lin frowned. "I don't get it."

"I'll do a flash spectrum on this residue while you're debriefing with Captain Larsen. That may tell us something," volunteered Tandy. "We're just about through here."

They were silent for a moment, watching the three technicians, Aseto, Foran, and Mayer, finish securing the repair craft. In another moment Mayer turned to report the job completed, and the three made their featherweight way to the entry, Mayer bound for his duty station, Foran and Aseto for the suit locker to store their pressure suits.

"You'd better get down to Larsen's office; he'll be waiting to hear your story," said Tandy as he and Lin, after a last careful look around, also left the compartment.

"Yes, I suppose so," replied Lin. "Would you stow these for me?" He held out his pressure suit, helmet, and gloves.

"Sure."

"Thanks. Larsen is going to want to know what caused the trouble out there, and I can't tell him. If you find anything odd about that spectrum, let us know right away, won't you?"

They separated, Lin heading for the central shaft to go down to the P and P Office on E-deck, Tandy for the lab in the ship's repair shop on G-deck, where he would vaporize a tiny bit of the residue on the wiping cloth with a laser beam and record the spectrum of the incandescent gas on film by means of the spectrophotometer. This "emission spectrum," so-called because the light waves photographed would be those emitted by the glowing gas, would provide a "fingerprint" of the elements present in the residue, each element causing its own narrow, bright band or bands at known wavelengths of the spectrum.

Lieutenant Lin descended the shaft to E-deck, falling slowly aft along the handrail, then squeezing it to arrest his eight-pound bulk opposite the air lock. Passing through the double doors, he was just in time to catch a glimpse of Aseto's stocky form turning into the recreation compartment doorway. Thinking of the rec room, he was suddenly thirsty, and decided that Captain Larsen could wait another minute while he got a drink of water. He moved on down the passage and pushed through the light polyurethane panel marked "Recr."

The room occupied a quarter of E-deck, its twenty-four-foot convex inner wall paralleling the sixty-three-foot concave outer one thirty feet away. Several hundred book-tapes ranging from *Aesop's Fables* to the *Teachings of Zoroaster,* the ancient Persian philosopher, filled shelves to the right of the door. To the left was a dispensing unit that offered a choice of water, milk, coffee, or cola from thin plastic tanks that were replenished directly through the wall behind the unit, beyond which was the mess hall–kitchen compartment. The recreation room furniture, also constructed of fragile looking plastics, included inflatable easy chairs and couches and molded straight chairs and tables. Along the other side wall were a stereo sound system and tape library, a game cabinet, a readout panel that showed the year, month, date, day, and hour in terms of Earth time, and finally a cabinet containing a projector and films, the roll-up screen for which hung from the ceiling at the inner end of the room. The long, concave outer wall was unobstructed and bore large, colorful reproductions of four of man's early ideas of the universe.

On the left was the Chaldean Earth-island surrounded by oceans hemmed in by unscalable mountains on whose towering shoulders rested the arch of the sky, studded with stars.

Next came the Egyptian version, somewhat similar in that the habitable Earth was ringed by huge, impregnable mountains along one shoulder of which the sun rode from east to west on a celestial river. The Egyptian sky, however, was a flat cover full of holes through which the stars were let down at night and drawn up during the day.

The third figure was the familiar zodiac with its twelve constellations and fanciful creatures in gold and red, blue and white.

The fourth universe, still geocentric, or having the Earth as its center, was that of the sixteenth-century Danish astronomer Tycho Brahe. His concept had advanced to allow all the planets except Earth to revolve around the sun which, with the Moon, revolved around the Earth.

Unfamiliar and striking as they were, the four illustrations of ancient astronomic notions drew far less attention than the twelve-foot stretch of transparent plexite in the center of the wall, for the metal sheathing outside was retractable, affording a view of the real thing. When outside radiation permitted, this window on the stars was bared.

As Lin came through the door he saw that Aseto was already back at one of his interminable chess games with the red-headed Cohen, taking up where he had left off, it seemed. Both men looked up in surprise.

"Don't mean to interrupt," said Lin quickly. "I'm after a drink, is all."

"Oh, that's all right, sir," responded Cohen innocently. "I thought maybe this dumb mechanic here had left the launching hatch open."

"Your move," was Aseto's only rejoinder.

With a smile Lin got his drink and left, regretting for

some obscure reason that none of the junior officers ever made fun of him that way. Rapping on the P and P office door, he entered.

"Sit down, Lieutenant." Captain Larsen fixed his light-blue eyes on Lin. "Navigation tells me L-5 is operational. What was the trouble?"

"The number-one harness was burnt off just back of the male half of the plug-in, sir. I have given Lieutenant Tandy some of the charred residue to do a flash spectrum. It looked like a short circuit had occurred between the cable and the mounting collar, but that seems unlikely with two inches of high vacuum to jump. The deck plug was not damaged, but there is a ragged, quarter-inch hole melted through the collar near the top, a definite thermal perforation, sir, with sputter deposits around it. I hope the spectrum shows something to give us a clue — I can't understand how it happened."

"Very good, Lieutenant. Let's hope so. It is unfortunate" — Larsen's eyes were suddenly icy — "that your thorough observation of details seemingly did not extend to operational procedure. Navigation also reported that your craft was occluded for eleven minutes by the cargo carrier, without warning or explanation. Was there some justification?"

"No, sir." Lin could feel his cheeks stiffen. "I was not aware of it. There was no reason for it, sir." Thinking back frantically, he recalled that he had forgotten to tell

Foran to take a directional fix on the *Pegasus* after he himself moved the cargo sled back away from the A-C. He must have cut off laser contact between the other two as he did so.

"You had a man in the repair craft at all times?"

"Yes, sir."

"You know that the auxiliary craft have remote operational capability, not only for the navigational convenience of using the spaceship's superior ranging and calculating equipment, but also as a safety factor for the personnel?" Larsen's voice was still hard but not quite so biting.

"Yes, sir."

"Very well. Never let it happen again." a wintry smile relaxed the Captain's visage. "Now go down to the lab and get busy with Tandy. We've got to find out what caused that harness to burn out."

"Yes, sir." Despite his chagrin and his bruised ego, he felt compelled to add, "I'm sorry I gave the department a bad mark, sir."

"Well, Lieutenant," Larsen's smile was warmer, "I guess the department can take its medicine."

Lin resolved as he left that he would not be the one to write the prescription for any more departmental medicine.

# 15

THAT FIRST grim night after the repair of the L-5, Foran thrashed and turned, his terribly disturbed mind struggling to heal the traumatic shock it had suffered. It was in vain. Foran woke from a nightmarish doze shortly after midnight, firmly convinced that they must abandon the projected landing on Mars or face certain disaster, the nature of which was hidden, along with its cause, behind the blank wall of his lost memory. Seen in that distorted light, the expedition had become for him a catastrophe-in-the-making that would justify almost any action to halt it, and the need to pierce the curtain of his amnesia took on renewed urgency. Somewhere in the events of that brief ride must be the proof he needed to convince the Commander to abandon all thought of landing on the red planet.

Two hours later — the sour taste of nausea in his throat from the knifelike throbbing inside his skull — he gave up. He could not remember. If he were going to save the expedition it would have to be by some means other than convincing the Colonel to turn back, for he had nothing to offer but vague forebodings.

Driven by the overriding need to halt what he was certain was a lethal course of events, he began to contemplate the possibility that he might have to act alone. Once his shock at the enormity of the notion wore off, the idea took root in the fertile soil of Foran's disturbed mind like a fire in dry grass. Somehow he must devise a deception that would prevent the Martian landing.

Sitting on the edge of the bunk he tried to approach the problem logically. Tampering with any of the ship's vital functions was out of the question — that much he knew — for the *Pegasus* was unavoidably committed to the use of Mars's gravitational field as a part of her total energy system. Her own power supply was incapable of exerting the massive short-term thrust required to stop her in relation to Earth and start her back toward it, even if her structure and contents could have stood the strain. This meant that the shortest way home was the long journey to Mars, where that planet's gravity could be used as a sort of sling to grasp the speeding ship, whirl it about, and start it back home. For the crew to survive the extended voyage it was obvious that power, guidance, and life-support systems must remain functional.

So his task, then, was to stop only the actual landing. Lying there, haunted by the certain knowledge that they must not land on Mars, frightened by the opaque curtain of forgetfulness that hid a portion of his day, Foran clenched his jaws in desperation. If only some supernatural force would intervene in a way that would make it impossible to carry out the mission.

All at once he sat up, clutching the edge of his bunk to keep his seven pounds from sailing halfway across the room. Suppose such a force did intervene! Not actually, of course, but suppose he could concoct a sufficiently convincing message from a superior being, requiring them to cut short the expedition. After all, no one knew when contact would be made with other, more-advanced life forms as man began to venture beyond his own doorstep.

A glance at his watch showed better than three hours yet to go of his "night," a theoretical term in interplanetary space where the shrunken, yet brilliant sun shines eternally in a black sky. Propping his aching head between his palms, Foran set about exploring the possibilities of his idea.

The only form of extraterrestrial contact he could hope to simulate would be a message of some sort, and here his familiarity with communications and his friendship with the two technicians could be helpful. He was pretty certain he could plant a message in the incoming traffic without being detected. It remained only to manufacture one that would carry conviction.

The thing would have to be done promptly, though, for it was common knowledge that the ship would be turned about to begin deceleration two days hence, in order to bring its velocity within the solar system down below 18.1 miles per second. 15 miles per second was the speed at which Mars was traveling around the sun and the additional 3.1 miles per second was the escape velocity for matter in Mar's gravitational field. To make contact with their initial goal, Phobos, they must join its 3700-mile-high orbit at matching speed, 4800 miles an hour relative to the Martian surface.

"All I have to do," thought George, "is to get them worried enough to put off deceleration for maybe one day, then they won't be able to slow down soon enough to stay in orbit."

By the time the light came up in his small room and the cheery music that normally wakened him came on, Foran had his plans laid and the message composed. A cold shower and a brisk toweling took care of most of the outward signs of his fatigue.

During his time off that day he showed up as usual in the communications center to ask questions and to study circuits and components. And, also as usual, he had had the willing help of both Joe Lane and Ned Thomas, who were glad to encourage his interest in communications. Only the meticulous Lieutenant Delatt had objected to the continuing unauthorized visits until his superior, Captain Sims, gave his approval as communications officer.

If Foran's questions were more concerned than usual with certain details of the maintenance schedule, such as how often and for how long the receiver was shut down for inspection, no one but Foran himself thought anything of it. He left earlier than usual that day, ostensibly to look up a point of theory in the recreation room library. Both Aseto and Cohen recalled later that he had also used the microtape writer on which personal letters back to Earth were prepared for transmittal by any who wished to do so.

At four o'clock he began his afternoon watch, which included for that day an inspection of the electronic warning and safety devices on B-, C-, and D-decks, as part of their maintenance schedule.

# 16

"WELL, IKE, D-day tomorrow."

Tip Reagan eased across the room and propped a big corner of his big frame on the edge of Colonel Sanborn's bed. The look of stern reserve that was his on-duty face gave way to a relaxed grin.

It had been precisely 8:01 P.M. when the raw-boned, muscular Executive Officer rapped and entered, putting a stop to Sanborn's perusal of the section reports, dispatches from mission control back on Earth, and other written information that had piled up during the day under his private access code in the computer's storage. Finishing the item on the screen, he touched his fingertips to the frame at the point where the word "off" was lettered. Obediently the viewer went off as a sensitive electromagnetic field responded to the nearby hand by activating a tiny microswitch. Thousands of similar proximity switches were used throughout the ship, for they were far lighter and faster acting than mechanical switches and equally dependable.

Sanborn hitched his chair back, blinked, and swung to face Reagan, his welcoming smile not quite wiping out the fine tracery of tension lines that shaded the corners of his eyes and mouth.

"Major, for a human being, even a superior human being such as yourself, to be so precisely punctual, day after day, is — well, if you were any good at mathematics we could have saved all that weight of computing equipment." The gleam in the Commander's eyes robbed the observation of any previous criticism.

"All I need is one more job around here!" exploded Reagan in mock outrage, his own blue-black eyes twinkling behind their ferocious glare. "I suppose next you'll want to put me out in back of this barrel to kick my feet so you can leave the Kresch drive behind, too!"

"Ha!" Ike laughed in spite of himself. "I'll bet you could do it, you muscle-bound mick!"

Tip was secretly pleased. He had been at some pains to knock on Sanborn's door at the same instant each evening, knowing that the latter would notice it and be diverted, if only for an instant, by something inconsequential and therefore relaxing.

For his part, Sanborn was also covertly pleased at what had to be a deliberate effort on the part of his husky Exec to provide a daily diversion. It was proof of the good state of Reagan's own morale. Leaning back and crossing his arms, Sanborn responded to his friend's original observation.

"Yes, tomorrow we begin deceleration, right around 9:25 A.M."

They had reached a point almost halfway from Earth to Mars and their foot-and-a-half-per-second acceleration must now be exerted in the opposite direction to slow them sufficiently to attain orbit when they got to Mars.

"Have Hewes and Larsen finished testing the carrier reversal programs?"

"No, but they were on the ninety-fourth one when I left," replied Tip. "No problems yet."

"Good! Mission control wants a microtape rerun of the test telemetry as soon as we finish. I guess they're still shaken up about that L-5 thing."

A probable solution had been found to the puzzle of the short-circuited wiring harness that had disabled the cargo carrier. Included in the emission spectrum of the tarry residue scraped from the socket had been hard evidence of the presence of metallic elements found in the springs used to hold the harness plugs firm in their sockets. The log of the work party that had assembled L-5 was no help, but the man who had installed the plug in the interface receptacle recalled that a spring had snapped out and, he thought, had been lost in orbital space as he was testing it. How a piece of that spring had become jammed between the cable and the housing, and later had worked its way into the live wire, would never be known, but there could be little doubt that it had, to its own fiery destruction and the temporary disablement of L-5.

"Excuse me, sir," said the speaker beside Sanborn. "Captain Sims calling you, urgent. He'll be using your private channel."

The voice and face were those of Colonel Sanborn's one-man office force, Chief Cyrus Rowe, whose round, placid features and baby-blue eyes masked a quick, efficient mind. Rowe also served as orderly to Major Reagan, and perhaps his most appreciated attribute was a certain hard-to-convince tone and manner with those who thought it necessary to break in on what little privacy his two bosses permitted themselves.

Sanborn knew and appreciated this loyalty. However, he also knew that young Captain Sims was not likely to act from ill-considered motives. It had been Sim's cool-headed courage and assistance that had enabled Sanborn to snatch him, together with an unconscious Tip Reagan, from the hungry edge of the abyss some three years ago, when their power plant had failed and left them marooned in lunar orbit in a leaking spacecraft.

"Thank you, Mister Rowe," he said. "I'll take it."

Touching a finger to the appropriate square of the panel before him he avoided Reagan's sharp glance, keeping his eyes on the screen as Rowe's image was replaced by that of Sims, slimmer and wearing a troubled frown and a strange, uncertain look.

"I'm sorry to trouble you, Colonel, but we have just received a message purporting to come from a source other than terrestrial, warning us to circle Mars and head back to Earth — or be destroyed."

Sanborn swallowed a crazy impulse to laugh. Sim's words were intelligible, but their collective sense was so utterly ridiculous that he simply stared back into the Captain's blue-gray eyes for three or four seconds, as though waiting for him to continue with some statement that would contain the key to an otherwise foolish riddle.

"I can put it on your screen if you wish. It's less than one frame long," added Sims, clearly aware that the Commander was as incredulous as he had been — still was, for that matter.

Tip Reagan had come up beside Sanborn. Now he reached out and turned on the Commander's alternate viewer, setting the channel selector to show the communications center. There was Sims, looking into the intercom viewer at a tiny replica of Sanborn's head and shoulders, while Technician Ned Thomas sat at the operator's post before the main LETWAVE unit, his blond head turned toward the Captain. No one else was in the room, and the door was closed, so no one was forcing Sims to speak.

Sanborn flicked a glance at the alternate screen, then looked back at Sims.

"I find it difficult to accept this as genuine, Captain," he said finally.

"Yes, sir," replied the Communications Officer, his tone and expression implying a full measure of agreement with the Colonel on that score. "It came through on the end of this evening's message block from mission control. Mister Thomas alerted me when it showed up on the readout, and I thought you would want to be called at once. Thomas has verified that it came through after the end-of-message signal, by the way."

Sanborn and Reagan exchanged a suspicious glance at that.

"I'm coming down there, Captain," announced Sanborn. "Make me a tissue of that message, and keep this to yourselves for the time being."

Signaling Rowe, he informed him of his intended destination, then rose and turned to his Executive Officer.

"Go up to the bridge, Tip. Find out if anything odd has happened in the last hour or so that might tie in with this, but don't say anything about it yet, not even to Frank Hewes. Look at the scanner log too. The whole thing is preposterous — it has to be — but we'll have to be sure there are no LGMs out there."

LGMs were the Little Green Men who hung around out in space to foul up things for unsuspecting astronauts. The term, borrowed from British radio astronomers years earlier, and by them from even earlier fiction writers, was still in popular use.

"Come down to communications when you get through," he finished, heading out the door.

# 17

THE REGULARITY of shipboard routine had been a major factor in making possible George Foran's successful insertion of his bogus message into an incoming transmission from Earth. Aside from a few places such as the recreation room, the living quarters, and the "torture chamber" where everyone had to put in two twenty-minute exercise periods a day, it was easy to predict who would be where and when. It was easy, too, to open the service plate that covered the point where the lead-in from one of the antennae came through the hull into the ceiling of a long, narrow storage room on C-deck. Full of bionics lab supplies and equipment, the storage room was never visited after supper.

Shortly after six-thirty George entered the L and R

compartment on B-deck and called in to report himself
beginning his regular inspection. The big chamber was
vacant, as he knew it would be at that time of day. On
his left the four A-Cs glinted in the subdued light. On
the opposite side were the shadowy tunnels of the aisles
between the spare-parts bins.

In point of fact, George's inspection was confined to
a few minutes of searching up and down rows and to a
few close looks with his flashlight before he found what
he wanted. Then he hurried out through the airlock and
down the shaft.

A few minutes later he was on tiptoe in the back corner
of the C-deck supply closet, hastily removing the inspection panel that concealed the antenna base with its
circuit-testing plug-in receptacle. From his pocket he
pulled a test plug, borrowed from one of the bins on the
deck above. Several fine wires of different colors led from
the back of the plug, and these he connected painstak-
ingly to certain terminals on a small plastic case also
acquired from spares — a portable transceiver. Twice he
had to stop to rub eyes blurred with exhaustion, but
finally the last connection was tightened.

His watch showed but a few minutes before seven
o'clock as he reached into a shirt pocket and pulled out
a thin, flexible strip. Quickly he inserted it in a slotted
little device on one side of the transceiver. The micro-

taped message was now ready to transmit when George pushed the button.

But the time for that step was still over an hour away, and the most difficult part of his preparation was yet to come. He must connect the portable set into the antenna lead, by inserting the test plug into the waiting receptacle, without the act being detected in the Communications Center — an impossible feat if the receiver there was on. The tremendous amplifying power of the long-range equipment would turn the tiny fluctuation of potential, caused by plugging in, into jagged peaks and valleys that would cause the automatic monitoring circuit to signal for human attention and undoubtedly would lead to an inspection of both antennae.

Here Foran's questions regarding communications center routine had provided the key to success. He had found that at precisely seven o'clock Lieutenant Delatt commenced a meticulous check-out of the receiving unit, always in the same way. Shutting off the receiver, he would run his fingers over the component units of integrated circuitry, feeling for any hot spots that might indicate an incipient breakdown. During the two minutes he was thus occupied the receiver was dead, and Foran could plug in his transceiver without fear of discovery. At one minute past seven he did so, turning it on to receiver mode and tucking it out of sight on top of a tall utility case that stood on end at the rear of the closetlike room.

Moving with cautious speed, he made his way back to the L and R compartment unobserved, called in to report his inspection of it completed, and went openly out across the main shaft and into the living quarters that were next on his schedule. In the passageway he met John Pryor.

"What are you doing, George, giving up sleeping? You look like you've been awake for a week."

Pryor was the one who had been witness to his discomfiture at the hands of Lieutenant Munn the other day. George knew he would have been embarrassed if he hadn't been so tense and exhausted.

"Hi, John."

He forced himself to speak casually to fend off the other's attention, for he had no time to spare. Pushing on, he completed his round of B-deck just after 7:30 P.M. and descended to C-deck, which was divided into two large airtight compartments in which were housed the bionics lab, the gymnasium, the infirmary, Dr. Finberg's office, and the forward stabilizer pairs, mounted with their working axes along the ship's Y- and Z-axes of motion. Sandwiched between the bionics lab and the gym was the narrow supply locker in which Foran had carried out his earlier preparations.

For the second time that evening he cheated on a compartment inspection, slipping out of the lab and into the supply room before five minutes of eight. A faint frying hiss came from the speaker as he eased the volume up to an audible level. The time was now just four minutes before eight, and two minutes before the evening transmission was due. Settling himself solidly, a finger on the switch that would activate the transmitter, he waited for the little string of dots that would begin the message and furnish synchronizing data to the antenna and receiver system. The transmission of "payload" data, the actual message, would begin one second after the dots had settled into a long, uninterrupted-sounding dash. This dash would continue until one second after the end of the last message, broken only by a microscopic pause on the heels of the last data bit, marking the end of the message block. It was this tiny interruption, no more than a click really, that would be Foran's signal to act. Fortunately he had listened to live sonic versions of several transmissions in the communications center and knew what to expect, for he had only that one second of unmodulated carrier wave at the end of the message, a standard interval that was part of the system's geometry, in which to insert his own quarter-second of compressed data by pushing the transmit button.

Shoulders hunched and eyes narrowed, he waited for the high, sharply defined notes — and suddenly they came! A dot, another dot, three or four more closely spaced, then the sound was continuous and George leaned forward, holding his breath, a tense index finger taking up the slack in the transmit button. Closing his eyes, he concentrated on the flow of that thin band of sound, like a narrow ribbon, through his head. Then almost of its own volition, his finger jabbed and released as the ribbon of sound was creased by a fractional pause, then ended.

It was done! The microtaped message over which he had labored — adding, deleting, even combing the dictionary for more impressive terms — the message was now included in the stored transmission in the communications center, awaiting readout.

The dry hiss of "grass," background noise from the transceiver, ceased as George snapped it off and pulled out the test plug, knowing that right now was the safest time to disconnect, while the duty operator one deck below was occupied with taking off the message just received and the big receiver was on standby. Hurrying now, he replaced the inspection plate over the antenna base, disconnected the test wires of the plug from the transceiver, removed his bit of tape from the reader, and went across to the bionics lab to call and report his inspection finished. With him he took the things that had to go back to the L and R compartment.

The call completed and his time and whereabouts officially if not truthfully accounted for, he crossed to the main shaft access door where he squinted through the view plate into the shaft. Seeing no one in the restricted field of vision, he eased the door open a crack and peered upward, just as someone started to open the B-deck door opposite L and R. Closing his own door he shrank back as the Commander himself slowed down and left the big tunnel by the door directly opposite.

"I wonder why he's going in there?" thought Foran impatiently. "If he got the message he should be going to D-deck, if anywhere."

Suspicious, he waited. In less than a minute, Colonel Sanborn emerged and went on down the shaft to the D-level. With a little grimace at his narrow escape, George peered out again, then stepped out onto the small landing. A brief glance down disclosed two fore-shortened figures at F- or G-level, and he hesitated no longer. Gripping the portable transceiver, he thrust himself up and ducked into L and R long enough to restore the borrowed equipment, after which he was free to return openly to C-deck to complete his inspection.

# 18

COLONEL SANBORN stood in the communications center rereading the message that his communications officer had handed him. It read:

*IPT-1, your science and your people are not ready to colonize other worlds. Your civilization has been watched for many centuries. It is substandard for interplanetary propagation. Only temporary visits by small exploration parties will be allowed during this century.*

*Since you cannot turn around and go back, you will shape your course and velocity to circle the planet you call Mars and return to your home planet. This is an order and will be enforced by your destruction if necessary.*

GALACTIC COUNCIL PATROL

On the way down from his cabin Sanborn had de-termined to de-emphasize the situation as much as possible, not permitting it to disrupt the increased tempo of activity attendant on tomorrow's reversal of the space-craft and cargo carriers. Now he choked back sudden suspicion and irritation provoked by the cavalier, peremp-tory message. Something about it wasn't right, was too pat. But — one step at a time, he reminded himself.

"Could this have originated on board?" he asked, looking up at Sims with a disbelieving frown.

"Yes, sir, but that wouldn't have been easy," replied the latter, "I was talking with Thomas about it while you were on the way down. To begin with, the message did come in through our receiver on the regular channel, immediately following the end-of-transmission signal from Base 1. It was tied into the routine store-and-read sequence, which could be done just as easily from Earth or the Moon as from here. I've sent word for a rerun of the whole message block to see if this will repeat." Sims hesitated, then added, "There is this, too. Whoever sent it almost has to be using our kind of hardware and tech-niques. You know, microtaping, pulse modulation, things that would affect the way our equipment handled the message —"

"Knowledge and hardware available, presumably, only back on Earth and here aboard this ship, you mean," broke in the Colonel.

"Yes, sir, but hard to use from here without detection."

"How long before the repeat transmission from mission control can be expected?"

"We're almost exactly five minutes' signal time from Earth. Another five minutes for the return, say two minutes for compliance at their end — " Sims glanced at the chronometer on the panel. "My signal is just arriving, so we should hear in seven minutes."

"All right," responded Sanborn impersonally, an abstracted frown on his face. "Where, in or on the *Pegasus,* could one add to an incoming signal?"

"Anywhere on the outer hull that afforded a line-of-sight shot into the mirror of either antenna, with a portable pulse transceiver set at the right frequency. Then one would need a message tape — which could be made on the microwriter in the recreation room." Sims's eyes glinted at the simplicity of that part of the operation, and he shifted unconsciously to the personal pronoun. "He could advance the tape a little, run his message on, advance it a little more, cut out the piece with the message on it, and splice the rest back together. Someone is always breaking a tape; it would be impossible to trace. That part would be easy."

As the Captain paused for breath, Colonel Sanborn broke in again.

"So the message could have been manufactured and from right here on board."

"Yes, but —"

"But what, Captain?"

It was clear to Sanborn why the younger man was loath to see the possibilities narrowed, for if the message were the work of someone aboard, that person would have to have certain factual knowledge and special skills — and the prime suspects would have to be the personnel of the communications section: Captain Sims himself, Lieutenant Delatt, and Technicians Thomas and Lane.

After the barest hesitation, Sims responded.

"But it could have been sent from Earth, or it could even be genuine — not that I think it is, but we can't rule out that possibility yet, can we?"

He was clearly not about to allow suspicion to center on his section exclusively, and Sanborn admired him for it.

"We can't rule out anything yet, and we must be sure to take in all the possibilities before we do start ruling out. Let's go on. Where, besides the antenna, could anyone tamper with incoming signals?"

Sanborn included Technician Thomas in his questioning glance, not because he expected the young man to know as much about the theory of the installation as Sims did, but because he was one of the four who must keep the matter confidential, and it made good sense to include him in the effort to authenticate or discredit the message.

Encouraged by the Colonel's glance, Thomas was the first to reply.

"There's an inspection plate in both escape-hatch covers on this deck, sir, and two more on G-deck," he said dubiously.

"That's so," agreed Sims, "and it is possible to direct a beam into the antenna from G-deck, but the hatch airlock would have to be opened which would show on the condition panel, and the watch officer would check it on the video."

"That's true, sir," acknowledged Thomas.

"I don't see how anyone could tap in on the antenna inside the hull undetected. The head end of these long-range receivers is so fantastically sensitive that we'd know on the board here if someone were fooling around the lead-in, even if he could get at it without being seen." Sims looked up at the ceiling a moment in thought. "It is *possible* that someone on board did it, but he's damned clever."

As he finished, the faint hiss of the LETWAVE carrier signal was audible from the monitor speaker which Thomas had just turned on in preparation for the repeat transmission from Base 1. In its dry whisper was the faint echo of that crashing roar that made first-generation space communications via radio frequency all but impossible over any great distance. The three men fell silent, their attention fixed on the instrument panel.

In the few seconds before the message reached them Sims found himself picturing the long stream of microsecond modulating pulses that carried Base 1's message flowing toward them at the speed of light along the ten-megawatt tracking and carrier beam that followed the ship from OFSET. Like a stream of bullets from an incredibly fast machine gun, the half-million-mile-long string of photonic pulses would cover in five minutes the vast distance traversed by the *Pegasus* in as many days, each gradually diffusing blip a bit of information that the receiver would feed into its computer storage to be translated into messages. The compressed transmission would require only a matter of seconds, though the readout could take several minutes, depending on how many messages there were and whether they had to be printed or could be routed right into the computer storage.

A clear, high note came from the speaker and the watchers fixed their eyes on the panel, the Colonel more or less instinctively, since he knew only generally what any fluctuation in observed instrument readings would mean. Sims and Thomas, however, leaned forward in concentration, with a more exact knowledge of what to look for.

The signal lasted for about ten seconds, sounding to the unaided ear like a single, long, high-pitched tone, so close together were the individual sound pulses. For practical purposes this sonic reproduction of the high-speed message was useless because the physical characteristic and geometry of the speaker, designed for voice reproduction, were not responsive enough to resolve the individual bits, even by taping and retardation. When it stopped, though, the three men were conscious that there had been no audible interruption or change of pitch during the signal to indicate a postscript tacked on the end. So they were prepared in advance for the collective verdict of the other instruments that the transmission had been entirely normal and uninterrupted.

"I'll run off the end of it, sir, and see if we get that one again," said Thomas turning to the control panel.

They didn't. The last message in the repeat transmission was followed by the symbol marking the end of transmission, then there was only the unmodulated, soft glow of the cathode screen.

"Well, that proves it wasn't bootlegged into the original transmission, but not much else," observed Sims.

Just then the speaker, still on, emitted a short beep which, run through the translating mechanisms of computer and reader, turned out to mean: "Please advise why you wanted the rerun." It was signed by the Communications Officer, Mission Control.

Captain Sims faced the Colonel.

"Do you want to answer that, sir, or — ?"

His real question, of course, was whether the Commander was ready to let anyone back on Earth in on the weird situation that confronted them.

"Acknowledge it, reply to follow," Sanborn instructed Thomas. "I'm expecting Major Reagan any minute, and I want to talk with him before we go any further."

Stepping to the intercom he identified himself to Lieutenant Munn in navigation and asked for Captain Hewes.

"Have we completed the cargo carrier check-out, Captain?"

"Yes, sir, Wood has just finished the last one. I'd have called you but Major Reagan said he'd pass the word. He's on his way down now," replied Hewes.

"Then we're all set to switch to deceleration mode on schedule," said Sanborn.

"Yes, sir." replied the Navigation Officer.

"Thank you, Captain. That's all."

Reagan arrived then, carefully closed the door and looked questioningly at Sanborn after glancing at the others.

"It's all right, Major, you can talk. Did you find anything interesting?" asked the Colonel, sensing that Reagan did not know how freely he could speak. "For the moment we've no secrets from one another about this thing. Are there any UFOs out there watching us?"

Though he asked the question in an intentionally joking manner, Sanborn was aware of a subdued tingle in the hair at the back of his neck, as though each follicle were drawing itself together to spring erect if Reagan answered in the affirmative.

"There is no evidence of anything out there, sir, not even a stray meteor or asteroid of any size. No detectable electromagnetic emissions that aren't naturally accounted for, either. I had Lieutenant Munn do full spherical sweeps for both radiation and reflection." Reagan paused for breath, then continued, "There's nothing unusual in the log either, and no one's had anything odd come to to his attention, as far as I could discover without being obvious about our problem. And the cargo carrier checkout is complete and OK," he added as a postscript.

"Thank you, Major. We've gotten no further here, except to confirm that the message was recorded on our normal Base-1 frequency at one minute before eight, apparently tacked on the end of a regular transmission, after the end-of-message signal. It did not repeat in a rerun of the same message block just now." The Colonel spoke quickly. "We know it must have included the access code for the store-and-read sequence, and that it began with our call letters, IPT-1, which sets it apart from the message preceding it, by implication if not by origin. Those are the facts. What do you make out of them?" he finished, looking around the small group.

The three looked at one another, and Reagan, after an instant of knitting his brow, spoke out.

"I think we could almost say that whoever sent that —" the Major swallowed some ill-advised word, in recognition of his duty as an officer and a gentleman to set Thomas a good example, and went on, "that insulting communication, knows a great deal about our technology — so much that he times his message to arrive just before we're about to start decelerating and tells us he knows we have to orbit Mars to get home. Well, how could anybody — or any intelligent thing — know all that if he weren't a human being tied up with the expedition in some way, either here on board or at the other end? Another thing — if we weren't going into temporary orbit with Phobos, we wouldn't have to start decelerating so soon," he added. "There's something funny about the timing of this thing."

Reagan ceased speaking and looked at the others in turn, as if challenging anyone to disagree. Thomas wore a thoughtful expression and Sims seemed satisfied with the Major's logic, but Colonel Sanborn, looking pleased, took up the discussion at once, as if he had been waiting for the Major to say just what he had said.

"You're right, Major, there most certainly is." He turned to Sims, "Captain, does the transmission from

Earth always begin on the split second according to schedule?"

"No, sir, it does not," responded Sims.

"All right, all messages travel at the same speed in space." Sanborn held up the message. "How did someone know when to start this message on its way to us so it would arrive just in time to slide in on the end of a transmission? To know that, he had to monitor the transmission, and the only place from which he could monitor and send it on time, other than the Earth and right here, would have to be somewhere between the two — if we assume the timing was deliberate, which I do. With all the terrestrial, lunar, and orbital tracking stations that are following us, such a position would mean certain discovery. This we will check on, because the absence of any foreign body between the Earth and us will prove the message is a hoax as far as I'm concerned, originating either from Earth or its immediate vicinity or right here on board." Sanborn paused, then smiled grimly.

"Lecture's over," he said, "unless you have something to add."

When no one spoke, he went on, abruptly becoming the Commander again by some subtle alteration of mood or attitude that Thomas could not define but found somehow reassuring.

"Mister Thomas, put in a call to mission control to alert General Charles for a message from me, code

3-A-4-S, on the stand-by channel. After you've made the signal, I want you to go up to L and R with Major Reagan. Make sure there are six portable transceivers there, one in each A-C and two in spares. If there aren't, you stay there, Tip, and send Thomas back. If there are, go over both antenna lead-ins. Check the service panels, examine any intercom and ventilation outlets they pass close to, any place they can be reached. Point out anything at all that is not exactly as it was when we left OFSET, Mister Thomas, even a scratch or dent you don't remember. Then —" Sanborn glanced at his Executive Officer, "look over the G-deck escape hatches from which a sender could have aimed a message at the antennae. Check the air-lock condition monitors for tampering. And remember, if someone aboard the *Pegasus* is behind this thing, he must be dangerously unbalanced. He will be looking for my reaction to the message, and he will probably have watched to see where I went and with whom I have talked. So be careful!"

Thomas turned to the console and got the Commander's message started on its fifty-five-million-mile journey back to mission control, while Captain Sims produced the antenna section plan, over which he and Reagan bent their heads in low-voiced conversation. Then Thomas finished and left, with Reagan, to carry out the inspection.

Sims, left alone with Sanborn, permitted a worried

frown to replace the look of disciplined reserve he maintained when others were present. To the admiration he felt for Sanborn as a man and astronaut was added the very personal feeling a man has for someone who has saved his life, and he affected the outward reserve to keep his private feelings from showing. He moved over to the intercom control and turned off the audio circuit to ensure that there would be no interruption while Sanborn was sending his message to the General. The video circuit would still allow them to see anyone who called in.

"Thanks," acknowledged the Colonel, seating himself at the transceiver. He poked a finger at a series of proximity switches that put the powerful set in transmit mode and selected the stand-by channel he planned to use. Then, on a small alphanumeric keyboard, he set up the key that would direct his message to the General's personal channel. Speaking with careful clarity, he identified himself, called the General, and specified the scrambler code, which he then entered on the keyboard before proceeding with the body of his message. This assured him of privacy since only General Charles and the Mission Control Officer knew the formula that would enable their receiver to unscramble the jumble of sound that followed. Explaining what had happened, Sanborn read off the peremptory injunction to give up the mission and return to Earth, then outlined briefly his thoughts concerning its validity and his plans for interim action.

"If I am right," he went on, "a sweep of our area by the tracking stations will disclose no casual objects large enough to be a source of a message, and we will then know that it is a hoax, origin either here or back there. For maximum assurance I ask that you arrange a sweep by the lunar observatory as well. I contemplate no change in flight plan or schedule. Only Reagan, Sims, Thomas, and I know of the message, and I plan to discuss it with Larsen, Hewes, Cardoza, Marcus, and Finberg, in confidence. Please confirm my handling or advise. End transmission."

As the Colonel finished and switched the set back to its receiving mode, the younger man spoke.

"There's something crazy about this, sir. Why would any human being do it unless he's insane? And if he is, how could he manage the technical end? I know it sounds nutty but, from that angle, the whole thing is a lot easier to accept on the assumption that it is genuine." Sims paused, then added almost defiantly, "After all, it's not impossible!"

# 19

B Y THE TIME Reagan and Thomas returned to the communications center it was nearly nine o'clock. The seven people already there took up most of the space not occupied by components of the LETWAVE system, but Reagan edged his way around and between them until he got close enough to Sanborn to let him know that they had found nothing. Thomas meanwhile pushed his way through to the console and relieved Sims.

"So you found nothing out of the way," observed the Colonel thoughtfully. "Strange. I felt sure you would."

"It may be there, sir. We were hurrying, you know, and a closer examination of things like the fasteners on the service and inspection panel covers might turn up something."

All five section heads were there: Larsen, Sims, Marcus — who tried to look put upon and kept tapping one foot as if impatient — Cardoza, and Hewes, in addition to Captain Finberg. Colonel Sanborn stepped back and cleared his throat.

"All right, gentlemen, I have shown you the message and given you my opinion of it," he said. "We have a preliminary reply from mission control, covering tracking stations only. They find no significant objects between them and us. To confirm that, General Charles is calling Tsiolnikov, President of the Astrophysical Institute, to get the lunar observatory to take a look with the big disk. Because I am convinced that they will confirm the negative report —" the Commander raised his voice fractionally, then lowered it, leaving everyone hanging on his next words, "we are going to proceed on the assumption that someone on board this spacecraft is insane enough to destroy us all. Until we know the truth, we can do no less."

Colonel Sanborn came to a full stop and stared somberly at each of them in turn, as if weighing their several abilities to comprehend the deadly possibilities of the situation. Even Marcus was still.

"I call to your attention," he went on coldly, "the fact that no one outside this room possesses authorized knowledge of the message or of anything that has taken place here tonight in connection with it. No one here pres-

ent" — the Colonel's usually pleasant voice held an un-
mistakable steely edge and his gray eyes were two chips
of flint — "is to disclose in any way, by word or action,
anything concerning the subject to anyone not now in this
room, under any circumstances. That," he said flatly, "is
an order, to be observed until countermanded by me or
by Major Reagan."

The Colonel waited long enough for his words to sink
in, and the silence was magnified by the faint sibilance
of the monitor speaker, whispering of sixty million miles
of space.

"To implement that order," he continued quietly, "you
will refrain absolutely from any reference to the matter
among yourselves anywhere except in the complete privacy of your offices, with your intercom audio turned off,
your door closed, and your voices lowered." Looking
around the circle of faces, the Colonel singled out
Thomas with a nod, and added, "You will have to use
the office of one of these other gentlemen if it becomes
necessary to discuss the matter."

"If you hear anyone," Sanborn spaced his words with
deliberate, icy distinctness, "anyone, here present or not,
refer in any way to this matter other than under the conditions I have established, you are to report it at once to
me or to Major Reagan, without alerting the party. Use
my personal intercom channel and remain within sight
or hearing of the individual until one of us arrives. If in

the meantime the safety of the ship is, in your opinion, endangered by the person's immediate actions, you are to restrain him, by using whatever force and means are necessary and reasonable. If you need help, you have my authority to call on anyone available."

The Colonel came to a full stop and looked about.

"Is there any question so far?"

A series of high-pitched dots from the speaker provided the immediate if unrelated reply, followed by the voice of General Charles, watery but understandable.

"This is General Everett Charles calling Colonel Ira Sanborn, Commander IPT-1, code 3-A-4-S —"

The Commander, with a quick "Excuse me, gentlemen," had moved to the console at the first thin beeps from the speaker. As the General's code reference came through, he pressed certain key numbers on the control panel to activate the proper unscrambling sequence, his interposed form concealing the panel as he did so. Then, donning a headphone set, he shut off the speaker and stood listening.

In the stirring about that followed, young Colonel Marcus caught the eye of Doc Finberg and muttered distinctly, "This is a lot of foolishness! We know the message is a fake, so why doesn't he just make an announcement, tell everyone. Then if it was done by somebody on board, he'll know that his crazy stunt didn't work and that everyone else will be watching for any more funny business." Marcus snorted. "Besides which, the nine of us can't keep watch over the whole crew!"

Finberg smiled noncommitally. He knew what Marcus's trouble was. It had far more to do with the Commander's ability to make the brilliant young astrophysicist feel commanded than it did with how he was handling the present situation. Brilliance, Finberg reflected, seldom dwelt with balanced maturity.

Reagan, who had overheard, had little use for the jejune intellectualism of the youthful genius, whom he called an "overstuffed technician who thinks Einstein is God and the Central Computer Complex is His Son." Now he scowled blackly at Marcus over Finberg's shoulder.

In a moment Colonel Sanborn hung up the headphone and turned to face them again.

"Well, that settles it," he said. "There is nothing out there that could have sent that message. Does anyone have a question regarding my instructions so far?"

No one did.

"Very well. We will now begin to eliminate those aboard the *Pegasus* who did not have the opportunity to do this thing, let alone the specialized knowledge. To begin with, we know, within a minute, when it was done and, within narrow limits, how and where it was done."

Glancing at his watch, Sanborn went on.

"Just over an hour ago, from one of the escape hatches

[147]

on G-deck, or from some point on one of the two antenna
lead-ins between B- and C-decks, that message was inserted into the evening transmission with a portable
transceiver using the tape adapter, obviously, since the
message was microtaped. We know from the signal duration that it was lapped over the last, unmodulated second
of the legitimate message beam, which was very clever,
and possible only if the sender were listening to the actual
transmission, all ready to push his transmit button in the
split second following the end-of-message signal.

That eliminates people such as Captain Sims and
Thomas, who might be prime suspects from the point of
special knowledge," — sardonic amusement glinted
briefly in the Commander's eyes — "but who were both
here at one minute of eight when the message was received. Larsen and Hewes were together in navigation,
working on the cargo carrier check-out —"

"With McPhee and Wood — and Major Reagan," in-
terjected Captain Hewes. "The Major left at exactly eight
o'clock."

"Yes," continued Sanborn. "That leaves Colonel Marcus, Major Cardoza, Captain Finberg, and myself, and
I was in my quarters when Major Reagan arrived there
at one minute past eight. The point being, gentlemen,
that it will be possible to prove very quickly that almost
everyone aboard could not have done it, on the basis of
opportunity alone. This you will do in the next half hour,

each for his own section, by casual conversation with your own personnel, while memories are still fresh and before the next watch takes over."

The Commander's glance again swept the group, lingering fractionally on Colonel Marcus.

"One more thing. We all hope, I know," he added soberly, "that the person responsible for this piece of criminal foolishness is back on Earth and that our precautions will be seen as having been unnecessary in retrospect. However, until he is apprehended, don't forget for a minute that there are a hundred ways he can cause us anything from serious inconvenience to total disaster, if he is on board. For that reason" — Sanborn spoke more quickly, a hint of impatience in his tone, — "we are taking no overt notice of his ultimatum because, one, he must not know it has been exposed and get alarmed, until we begin our deceleration maneuver on schedule tomorrow, and two, because I have no intention of provoking a crisis before we know whom we don't have to watch.

"Now, if any of you can help each other with personal knowledge of the whereabouts of people during the critical time, I suggest you do so before you leave. Make it quick, though, for I'll expect you in my quarters by nine forty-five, except for you, Mr. Thomas. Meanwhile, Major," the Colonel looked at Cardoza, "since I'll be needing Captain Finberg's advice, you'd better talk with him now. That's all, gentlemen."

No one moved or spoke for an instant. Then, as if released from a spell, they all began to talk at once. Captain Larsen was the first to leave, with Marcus and Hewes close behind. Waiting for Cardoza and Captain Finberg to finish, the Commander turned to his big Executive Officer.

"Was Rowe at his station when you came into my quarters this evening?"

"Yes," replied Reagan, "he was. When I came down the shaft from A-deck, there was only one other person in it going down at the F-deck level. It was Mayer. He and young Foran were doing the hull integrity inspection. I heard McPhee acknowledging their compartment checks."

"That is Larsen's department. He'll be talking with each of them before he comes up. What was our young genius grumbling about while I was listening to the General? I saw you looking very disrespectfully in his direction."

"Oh, he had a better idea, as usual. Someone ought to put him on report for unauthorized use of a dangerous weapon — that pop-off brain of his! He's just like a kid when he gets away from his neutron stars and precessions and theories."

Just then Captain Finberg crossed the room toward them as Major Cardoza left with a nod in their direction.

"Captain," asked Sanborn a few minutes later, the door

to his quarters safely closed behind them, "is it possible for one of my normal, well-adjusted, healthy crew, all with clean records, to become suddenly unbalanced? Or, to come at it a different way, is it possible for someone who has been unbalanced for some time to have fooled our experts and us?"

"Yes, to the former. Extremely unlikely but possible. As for the latter, I cannot believe it could happen, given the depth of information we have on everyone and the high level of competence of our astromedical staff."

"All right. In the former case, is there some one form of insanity, some readily recognizable syndrome, I believe you call it, that would tie in with what has happened here?"

"More than one," Finberg replied, "but not necessarily readily recognizable. This message could be the act of someone manifesting the Antaeus syndrome —" the Captain's eyes twinkled, "as a result of a conversion hysteria arising from a subliminal positive geotropism — suppressed homesickness for Earth, if you will. Actually, that would tie in very nicely, because the message is designed to get us to go there as quickly as possible, while the sender, if he is on board, is acting quite rationally otherwise, which is typical."

"A kind of space sickness?" broke in Reagan, never one for using two big words when one little one would do.

"You could call it that," agreed the physician.

"That would supply a motive, too," said the Colonel reflectively. "Something that is hard to think of for anyone back on Earth. Would a person in this condition become homicidal or attempt to destroy the ship to accomplish his purpose, knowing that he would die, too?"

"Let me talk to him for a half hour or so, and I'll have the beginning of an idea of how to answer that," smiled Finberg. "At the worst, yes."

"But he wouldn't be likely to act without provocation, would he? What I mean is, here we have this ultimatum which in effect gives us about twelve hours leeway, because, as I said earlier, this person cannot know that his scheme is not going to work until we do start decelerating on schedule. Now, will he abide by his own conditions and wait the twelve hours, or is he liable to go completely off his rocker and blow us up an hour from now?"

"The type of disorder I have reference to is characterized by, among other things, a meticulous adherence to plan and an exaggeratedly normal overt behavior. I believe you are following the best course in not publicizing the message. But how," added Finberg, "do you know that I didn't send it and that I won't destroy us all the minute I get a chance?"

Behind the half-humorous question, Sanborn could sense a genuine interest.

"Are you questioning my judgment, Captain?" he asked in turn, with an amused side glance at Reagan.

"A commander has to know these things. But I presume you would like some empiric evidence on which to base your continuing faith in my capability."

Finberg reddened and made as if to speak, but the Colonel, with a friendly smile, continued without pause.

"When I got that message it seemed probable, for several reasons, that I was confronted with the act of a mentally sick man, and I thought of you, Captain, in your professional capacity, of course. That reminded me in turn that Captain Spicer, the Chaplain, had left my quarters for your office some fifteen minutes earlier, to try to persuade you, as both a doctor and a Masorete, to speak at one of his Sunday services. On my way down to communications I stopped off at C-deck long enough to see that he was still with you. I hope he succeeded, by the way."

Reagan was struck again by his Commander's ability to compartmentalize his thoughts and feelings. Here they were, in the midst of a potentially lethal situation, and Sanborn, having done what he could for the moment, calmly involved himself in the padre's ecumenic endeavors.

The arrival of Captain Hewes soon put an end to their discussion, as he and the Commander conferred briefly over the details of the impending switchover to deceleration. Colonel Marcus came next, with Major Cardoza and Captain Sims close behind. Promptly on the mark of nine forty-five, Captain Larsen pushed his stocky nine and a half pounds through the door to complete the roster.

Colonel Sanborn's quarters were smaller in overall dimensions than the communications center, but because there was much less equipment, the room was not as crowded with seven extra men in it as the communications center had been. Sims, Cardoza, and Marcus sat along the outer edge of the bunk, Larsen and Hewes stood by the adjoining wall with Finberg opposite, and big Tip Reagan lounged across the doorway, one foot propped over the other instep and a brawny arm braced against the lintel, looking for all the world like a jailer guarding a party of prisoners.

Sanborn, swinging his chair around to face his desk, assured himself that the intercom sound was still turned off, picked up a pencil and swung back to face the room. He spoke, breaking the expectant hush that had fallen.

"Let's find out where we stand. Give me just the name of anyone in your section for whom you were not able to establish an alibi. Captain Hewes?"

"John Pryor, sir."

"Captain Larsen?"

"Lin, Foran, and Aseto."

In all, eight names appeared on the list, including those of four persons who were supposedly asleep, or at least in bed. Foran had called in from the bionics lab at six minutes past eight to report his inspection of it complete, and Sanborn, about to draw a line through the name, hesitated and went on without doing so. Excluding those abed and Foran, there remained three whose whereabouts had not been specifically witnessed by another.

John Pryor had probably been studying his beloved astrophysics in his quarters, as he was when Hewes walked by the door an hour and twenty minutes later. At least, so he stated in a conversation with the latter.

Joel Lane, the other communications technician in Sims's section, had probably been down in the P and P lab where, with Captain Larsen's permission, he spent a good share of his off-duty time using the fine new equipment to work out an idea involving a refinement in laser antenna design. As it happened, Larsen had looked in there just after eight o'clock, minutes before Sanborn first summoned the section heads to the communications center. The lab had been empty, though lights were on and a small gallium arsenide laser was set up on the bench, along with some other equipment that Larsen recognized as Lane's experimental antenna.

The third person lacking a witness to his whereabouts at the crucial time was Major Cardoza, who had been engaged in his nightly examination of the algae irradiation chamber from about seven-thirty until he was called to the meeting.

"I spoke to Parks on the way in; he was on duty in the

separator compartment. You have to go through it, you know, to get to the irradiator. But he was not there when I came out, so I have no way to prove I stayed in there."

The Major, it was plain to see, was not accustomed to situations that called for him to account for his where-abouts. His large, handsome face was a bit pinker than usual under its cap of curly black hair, and his brown eyes held a glint of controlled annoyance that was matched by the tone of his voice.

Sanborn bit back a twitch of amused sympathy that tugged at his lips and thanked Cardoza quietly.

"With no disrespect intended, Major," he added, "I doubt that you possess the specialized knowledge of com-munications techniques and hardware to make it reason-able to suspect you."

The Major managed to look obscurely comforted and discomfited at one and the same time, as though con-vinced of the logic of Sanborn's statement but displeased by the imputation of a lack of knowledge on his part.

"We cannot," continued the Commander, now speak-ing to them all, "say the same for Lane and Pryor." He looked down at the names he had written, then across the room at Sims. "What about this man Foran, Captain? Hasn't he been picking up a lot of information about your operation from Thomas and Lane on his time off?"

"Yes, sir. I asked Thomas about him before I came up. He is superficially familiar with our routine, and he had some communications training before the Expedition. And he worked with the communications section during assembly of the *Pegasus*. He might have done it, but it seems unlikely."

"All right, in he goes, along with Lin, Munn, Ardley, and Andy Lane — the other Lane — who were all supposedly sleeping."

Sanborn dropped his gaze to the paper, studied it intently for a moment, then centered it carefully on the desk and swung about.

"Good! Now I have one more task to impose upon you. Beginning tomorrow morning, Dr. Finberg is going to spend a half hour apiece with a random sample of ten men, retesting some definitive areas of their personality profiles, to see what effect the trip thus far may have had on them. At eight-thirty John Pryor will report to the Medical Officer —" and Sanborn proceeded, straight-faced, to name Joel Lane and George Foran as the second and third members of his random sample, followed by the four sleeping men for whom there was no proven alibi at the time the threat was received. To the seven names he added those of Captain Hewes, Major Reagan, and Colonel Marcus, "To balance the sample," he explained coolly.

"Whatever your thoughts may be concerning the personnel included in the sample," he went on, firmly overriding the impatient sputter from Marcus, "please reserve your remarks for the time being. You gentlemen whom I have named may arrange to see Captain Finberg after he has interviewed the others and after we have begun deceleration. The test, as Major Cardoza can tell you, is something that was scheduled to be done en route. This seems an opportune time for it. I shall defer announcement of the conferences until tomorrow at seven A.M., which means no discussion of the subject between now and the time my order goes out in the morning. For tonight, then, you will follow your normal routine, but tomorrow, between the time each of these men" — Sanborn tapped the list behind him — "is notified of his interview and the time he actually arrives in Captain Finberg's office, you will have to keep him under surveillance, so rearrange your duty rosters to that end and notify Captain Sims. He will have Mister Thomas checking intercom outlets in the appropriate areas during the morning, and Major Reagan or I will be about.

"One other thing. If you get definite proof that one or more of these names can be removed from the suspect list, call me at once.

"That is all, gentlemen. Doctor, will you stay for a moment?"

Reagan led the exodus from the room, waiting in the narrow corridor until they had all filed out, the frustrated Colonel Marcus bringing up the rear. Then the Major stuck his head back in and inquired, "Need me, sir?"

"No, but you'd better check with Sims. He'll be without Thomas and Lane from nine to nine-thirty in the morning. You may have to divert a man to him from another section for that half hour. Then see how Hewes is fixed. He'll have his hands full with the deceleration routine from early morning on. It's unfortunate that Pryor has to be involved in this, but it can't be helped. Then you'd better get some rest. Tomorrow will be a strenuous day."

As the door finally closed behind Reagan, the Colonel reclaimed his seat with a little sigh.

"Think you can pull it off, Captain?" he asked. "I know it's short notice and too little time for a Rorschach test or anything fancy, but how about that sensory-motor test, the one with the small circles and dots in patterns? Isn't that in everyone's P-file, and wouldn't it show up someone with a mental warp such as this man must have?"

Finberg looked suspiciously at Sanborn for an instant before replying.

"I think you're referring to the Bender-Gestalt type of test that is, as you said, taken by all space corps applicants and was redone for the personnel of the MAR-SET program, except for a few civilian experts like Larsen and Marcus. I think, too, that you know rather more about psychiatry than I would have expected — enough more so that I'll answer your two questions very briefly. Yes, I think I can pull it off if the man is one

[159]

of those I see in the morning, and yes, the B-G test should show him up, along with other behavioral factors and a graphology comparison to his previous norm."

A little of the tautness went out of the muscles around the Commander's jaw.

"Good! I'm sorry to spring it on you like that, but I could not be sure the number of men would be small enough to handle this way until the results were in. Thank you."

Sanborn rose to mark the end of the interview and saw the Captain to the door, where the latter tarried long enough to say:

"Colonel, as your doctor, I recommend that you throttle back and get a good night's sleep yourself. Goodnight, sir."

Whether it was the Doctor's advice or the knowledge that he had accomplished his initial aim of containing the attempted disruption of his schedule or a combination of the two, Sanborn went to bed shortly after eleven o'clock, expecting to drift off at once. Sleep, however, kept playing tag with him, ducking back just as he reached out for it. Finally he rolled out of bed and crossed to his desk, irked at the pointless parade of the evening's events that kept going around in his mind like a bad dream that refuses to end.

What had he left undone? Where could he have done differently? Had he been justified in including Marcus in his "random" sample of personnel to be tested, or had he been venting petty annoyance or even jealousy of the other's bland assumption of VIP status? Unquestionably the brilliant young astrophysicist was entitled to special consideration in such mundane areas of life as discipline, manners, and consideration for others, for his mind was apt to be light years away from his physical surroundings a good share of the time. Of course science, and eventually mankind, might benefit from the ideas he brought back, but Sanborn was not persuaded that a little more self-restraint on the part of Marcus would have any bad effects on the man's unique gifts.

"Anyhow," he thought, "it's my responsibility to see that we all get to Mars and back safely, and I can't take time to worry about whether someone's going to feel like obeying my orders. He'll have to get used to the idea, whether he likes it or not."

Irritated at himself for falling into this mood of restless uncertainty, the Colonel did an "armchair" inspection of the main compartments, switching from one to another on his video screen, looking for — what? It came to him suddenly that the cause of his wakefulness was worry over what the unidentified lunatic might attempt during the night. Exasperated, he rose with an abruptness that carried his light frame up off the floor and thumped an automatically raised hand on the ceiling.

"Look, knothead!" he told himself silently, "you've been through all this; you've made your arrangements, and they're adequate! Now, drop it! Whoever this poor guy is, he won't know his plan didn't work until we go into deceleration tomorrow."

# 20

C<small>APTAIN</small> L<small>ARSEN</small> elected to transfer Technician George Foran to the detail posted to L and R compartment maintenance the next morning, for two reasons. For one thing, that was where he himself was going to be. For another, Foran could better be spared from that detail for his half-hour session with Finberg than from his original assignment to power-plant inspection. The focused field C-N reactors of the power plant emitted some stray radiation, and that meant special clothes and the strip-and-scrub routine for everyone who entered the shielded door on which was stenciled the scarlet delta and atom danger sign.

"Cohen can swap shifts with you," said Larsen, watching the younger man closely as he told him of the reason for the changed duty assignment. "He was due tomorrow. You can take that shift."

It was the first time in two days that Larsen had happened to confront Foran at close range, and he noted right away that something youthful and vulnerable was gone from his expression, replaced by a secretive, hooded look. As a strongly independent man himself, Captain Larsen was readier than some to accord any man the right to the privacy of his own thoughts. Also he knew that Foran, as the youngster of the expedition, was the target of well-intended but sometimes caustic humor, and his own youth was not so deeply buried that he didn't remember resenting the inquisitive stares of his superiors at times. By the same token, the Captain was not apt to be fooled very often or his independence would not have paid off. He didn't miss the tight little ridges at the corners of Foran's jaw and the frequent, small hand movements, indicative of tension, as the young man stood before him waiting to be dispatched to his new station. Larsen wondered, finding it hard to conceive that this eager kid, as everyone thought of him, could be behind the scheme to upset the mission. Yet it was clear that something was bothering him. Captain Larsen determined to follow Sanborn's surveillance order to the letter until he turned Foran over to the doctor.

At eight o'clock, therefore, Larsen was busy in the L and R compartment, along with his work party. Ostensibly examining the oil-bath vane pump and foreline condensing trap used to evacuate air from the launching chamber, he was at the same time keeping a peripheral eye on Foran as the latter checked supplies and equipment aboard the four A-Cs, working with Aseto. At most, he was less than thirty feet away from the pair.

Chance and different work schedules had combined to prevent Ray Aseto from making good his resolve to speak with George about that unforgettable view of the *Pegasus* as they had seen it from the auxiliary craft on their way to the disabled cargo carrier. Working now in an A-C with Foran, he was reminded of his resolve.

"Hey, George," he said, "you remember on the way out to work on the L-5, just after we turned around to decelerate, what a wonderful picture the ship's thrust cone made?" Aseto looked up from the backpack he was checking, expecting to see an expression of pleased recollection on his companion's face.

Instead, Foran stared at him with a strange frozen look, half fear, half something else that Ray could not identify. Then he smiled brightly and replied.

"Yeah! Pretty, wasn't it!"

A premonition of trouble tugged at Aseto's mind, for the smile was put on and the words were forced. It didn't make sense, unless —

"He acts as if he doesn't remember." The thought startled Ray. "But that's ridiculous! The thing made a tremendous impression on him, just as it did on me. Perhaps he's embarrassed to talk about it now." The explanation was plausible but it did not satisfy Aseto, for George's reaction had been something other than mere youthful embarrassment — of that he was certain.

"Remember when you said, 'It's beautiful!' and our little gentleman, Lieutenant Lin, came back with 'Very impressive,' in that snotty way he has. I was so mad I just shut up."

While he spoke, Aseto watched the empty gleam in his companion's eyes for some spark of recollection, but he could detect none. The fixed smile, however, gave way to a look of forced concentration, as if Foran were having trouble following the words. Nor was the smile resumed when the young astronaut replied with a mono-syllabic "Yeah," then turned back abruptly to the tool locker he was checking. Aseto, annoyed and puzzled, began to embroider the facts.

"I think I got even with him, though, when I said I thought it was more than just 'impressive.' Remember how snippy he sounded when he said, 'Each of us is entitled to his own opinion, Mister Aseto'?"

"Yes, I remember."

Foran spoke without looking up, in the tone of one giving the obvious response without knowing the facts. A wooden, secretive expression was evident on his averted profile.

He really *doesn't* remember, thought Aseto, or he wouldn't have agreed to something that never happened. Aloud, he said, "Well, this isn't getting any work done, is it? I just wanted you to know I felt the same way you did about that thrust cone."

Without bothering to observe the effect of his words, Ray pushed the backpack into its slot and checked it off on the maintenance schedule. For a moment he considered reminding the younger man of the strict standing orders to report any indication of irrational behavior. But he did not want to make trouble, and the idea of playing stool pigeon, even potential stool pigeon, was so utterly foreign to Aseto's nature that he could not bring himself to speak. Besides, he remembered, there was that psychometric test Foran was about to take. If anything was wrong the test would show it up, whereas his own intervention might well lead to lasting enmity on George's part. Ray decided to let Doc Finberg cope with Foran's problem, whatever it might be.

Aseto was now checking a SCAT, a Self-Contained Auxiliary Thruster. Each A-C carried two thrusters for use in helping to move unwieldy objects about outside the ship, where their thick plume of scalding steam would do no harm as their twenty-five-pound shove helped overcome inertia. Shifting the portable thruster to a different position in his lap, Ray glanced around the compartment. Captain Larsen was crouched by the evacuating pump in a position that gave him a good view of the row of A-Cs. Thomas, from communications, was still peering and poking at the tiny sender module of one of the intercom pickups on which he had been working when the maintenance party arrived.

Just then the inner air-lock door, giving access to the great trunk of the main shaft, opened to admit the tall, lithe figure of the Commander himself. Seemingly in no hurry, he spoke a word to Thomas and moved on slowly, glancing about, until he reached Larsen's side. There he looked closely at something the latter pointed out, scrunched down and exchanged a few indistinguishable words with him, then rose slowly and sauntered over to lean both hands on the hatch coaming of the A-C in which Aseto and Foran were at work.

"Good morning, gentlemen," he greeted them with a friendly smile. "Don't let me interrupt; I'm just sight-seeing. How is our high-priced hardware holding up?"

Ray, usually taciturn, uttered the first words that came into his head as he saw an incredulous, frightened look sweep over Foran's features, as if he were seeing an apparition.

"Great, sir. I was just thinking we might as well have left most of that replacement stuff at home. We've only replaced one sensor and one switch since we left OFSET."

"That's good to hear," smiled Sanborn. "Let's hope it

continues." He turned away with a cheerful nod, spoke briefly to Larsen, and headed for the door.

Aseto stole a sidelong glance at his companion and found him gazing after the departing head of the expedition with the vacant stare of a person in shock, yet his hands were clasped so tightly that the knuckles were white.

"Now what?" thought Ray. "Why should just seeing the Commander knock him for a loop like that? And why didn't the Commander notice the look on his face — or did he?" Beginning to suspect that things of which he had no knowledge were taking place around him, he pushed the SCAT back into its wall bracket, checked the list, and started on "Tanks, Suit, $O_2$, 10 lb. (4)."

At that moment the harsh voice of the intercom rasped out:

"Attention all personnel! Attitude reversal will begin in ten minutes. All stabilization procedures finish by oh nine two five hours. Report by section. That is all."

In simple English this meant things had to be secured to stay in place as the ship pivoted. Most of this had been done by the preceding watch.

Larsen rose and came over to the open hatch.

"All right, Aseto, secure that for now. Make a note of where you leave off on the checklist. You can pick it up after we start the turn; you'll have half an hour before the counterthrust."

Counterthrust, a short burn of the attitude jets opposite those jets that had started the turn, would stop it when the ship had swung 180° on its X-axis and was pointing back the way it had come.

"Foran," went on the Captain, "you're due in Captain Finberg's office at nine-thirty. Leave that to Mister Aseto and take these inspection sheets down to the office for me. You can go right from there to Medical."

Foran gave no indication that he had heard.

# 21

Even before Captain Larsen spoke, Foran's mind was a blank. The night before, he had watched as first Sanborn and then his section heads had hurried to the communications center just after eight o'clock to emerge some time later. He had seen them all, still later, heading for the Commander's quarters, then departing all together, faces tight and uncommunicative. After that he knew that his message had gotten through, yet he hardly slept, waiting tensely for morning and word of a change in plans that would end all possibility of a Martian landing.

When the morning orders included no postponement of deceleration, Foran's headache returned, helped along by word of his selection to take the psychometry test.

When it got to be nine o'clock, with reversal scheduled to begin at nine-thirty and still no word of deferment, he was so tense he could hardly follow the simple steps of the maintenance check. Two or three times he found himself going over the same thing again and again.

Then Aseto had started to reminisce about something that apparently took place on the trip to the disabled cargo sled, and a new terror was added, for of course he had no recollection of it and had to bluff, hoping desperately that the other would not catch on and expose him.

When the Commander walked into the compartment at nine-fifteen, the tormented Foran had come within an ace of leaping up and screaming at him to know what was being done about the message. Numbly he watched Sanborn approach, make some inconsequential remark, and leave. Clenching his hands together to stop their shaking, he saw that Aseto was looking at him suspiciously, and he knew he must get to work again. Yet he knew, too, that if he tried to move, his control would shatter and something terrible would happen.

The terrible thing, the thing he must never even shape the thought of, was the failure of his plan.

But now time had run out, and the choice was no longer his to make. The raucous blare of the intercom bade him accept the unacceptable. Attitude reversal —

on schedule! Deceleration and the landing on Mars. His plan had failed.

Crouched behind the left-hand seat of the A-C with Aseto between him and the open hatch, Foran froze up — like a weapon with a faulty trigger and a live round in the breech, needing only a jar to discharge it.

"Mister Foran, did you hear me?"

It was the hard ring of authority in Captain Larsen's voice more than the words he spoke that set Foran off. With the speed of a striking snake, he flung himself out of the corner, upsetting Aseto and knocking him into Larsen. The two went down in a tangle, inspection sheets a swirl of tissues about them. A wrench which had been in Larsen's hand clanged on the deck.

"We'll all die if we land on Mars!" screamed Foran, his voice ragged with hysteria. "I've got to tell the Colonel!"

Snatching one of the two portable thrusters from its clamp, he sprang away from the A-C and headed for the door to the main shaft. Ned Thomas recovered from his shock and launched himself off to intercept.

Larsen, too, was up and scrambling after Foran, but too far behind to do any good.

"Get away!" shouted Foran hoarsely, pointing the nozzle of the thruster in Thomas's direction as their paths converged. For an instant Thomas hesitated, and Foran won out, slamming the air-lock door behind him and opening the one beyond. This prevented Thomas from following because of the interlock, a fact which Foran still seemed to realize, for he kicked off one sandal and reached down to wedge it between the door and the jamb. Then, as he stood up, the opposite door swung open and Major Reagan emerged onto the small landing. Catching sight of the wild-eyed, disheveled figure of Foran clutching a thruster as if it were a pistol, Reagan let out a shout and started around the peripheral catwalk linking both landings to the up-and-down stairway.

Instantly Foran levelled the thruster and squeezed the discharge valve wide open.

With a hissing roar, a geyser of steam filled the upper end of the shaft in seconds. It hid the choking Reagan who clawed frantically at the A-deck door to which he had hurled himself when he saw Foran pointing the thruster at him. It hid the hapless Foran, slammed against the door behind him by the full twenty-five-pound recoil of the thruster, equal in the low-gravity environment to three times his own weight. His fingers frozen on the thruster valve, Foran lurched as his bare foot slipped on the metal plate. Then he slid from the landing in a sharply accelerating curve around and down the smooth, wet wall of the shaft, into sound-filled darkness, as thick steam hid the lights.

The roar of the thruster ceased with a soft thud.

*     *     *

For the third time that morning Sol Finberg glanced quickly through the personal inventory section of an expedition member's file — that of George Foran. For the third time, too, he prepared himself to be sensitive, perceptive, understanding, sympathetic if need be — the qualities he needed to gain the man's confidence and co-operation. At the same time he would have to remain objective enough to avoid intuitive judgments and to interpret and use properly the information obtained from the man's words and actions. It was hard, demanding work, especially for one who was not a psychiatric specialist.

Neither Pryor nor Lane had shown significant deviation from their behavioral norms, nor did their motor responses seem erratic. Finberg would stake his career on his judgment that neither one had sent the threatening message. Laying out fresh blank sheets of paper for Foran to use in the drawing test, he dated and identified Lane's neat copy of the little designs of circles, dots, and odd figures and slid it into a drawer on top of Pryor's. Rising, he walked over to open the thin plastic door to the outer corridor. His next client wasn't quite due, but he might arrive early.

At that moment a barely perceptible tremor ran through the floor and Finberg stopped in the act of opening the door, head half raised. The sensation was akin to the quiver produced by a brief thrust of the attitude jets, a common enough occurrence in the week of station keeping before they left Earth orbit, but one that had not been felt since then because the imperceptible thrust of the gimbaled steering heads in the actinic drive maintained the ship's trim as well as its course. This sensation was different, though, and Finberg was just wondering what was responsible for the difference when the intercom clicked on and a sharply urgent voice rasped out.

"Attention! This is Colonel Sanborn! All hands keep out of the main shaft above easy deck!"

"Foran." thought Finberg, as the Commander continued speaking. "He was due next!"

Whirling, Captain Finberg got back to his desk, snatched the always ready medical kit from its place and was on his way out the door again.

"Come on, Joe!" he called to the big, blond medic, Joe Alley, who had risen from his desk in the infirmary and waited in the doorway.

# 22

COLONEL SANBORN stood on an E-deck landing in the main shaft, peering up at the door to the L and R compartment, waiting for Foran as he had for Pryor and then for Lane. This time, however, he had a hunch, a feeling of expectation. There had been something about the quick garrulousness of Aseto and the dour silence of young Foran that was out of character for both, almost as if they had swapped personalities. Of course it could be that they had quarreled about something, and Larsen had put them together without realizing it. There had been something in the air there, a tension hovering like an invisible mantle. And more over Foran than Aseto, if his hunch was correct.

"Have those two had a fight?" he had asked Larsen after his brief chat with Aseto.

"Not that I know of," the thick-set Captain had replied, in his sharp eyes an unspoken question.

"The wrong one did all the talking," had been Sanborn's cryptic observation as he left to take up his post in the long, gleaming tunnel of the main shaft.

Now, as he peered upward through the symmetrical maze of struts and braces, the sharp click of an opening door coincided with the abrupt appearance of a figure on the L and R landing. He craned to get a better view but the figure stooped out of his line of vision for an instant, reappearing as the sharp snick of a second latch reached his ears from somewhere out of sight above. For a split second young Foran's head and shoulders appeared over the edge of the landing, tense and motionless, and Sanborn's own muscles tightened, for he knew instinctively from the frozen rigidity of the other's posture that something had gone wrong.

First there was a flicker of motion at the shaft door opposite Foran, accompanied by a sharp hail — unmistakably Reagan — then a white jet stabbed out from Foran's side. Rebounding off the opposite side in a ballooning, explosive rush, it filled the top of the shaft with a roiling mass of steam to accompaniment of a roaring hiss that Sanborn recognized. Foran was using a thruster as a weapon, directing its scalding blast of steam at Tip Reagan! Giving an involuntary shout of his own, aware that the intercom was chattering, Sanborn caught himself in the act of leaping up the shaft into the billowing mushroom of gray vapor that came rushing down at him. Horrified, helpless to intervene, Ike cursed himself for not confining Foran at once, as the muffled roar of the thruster kept on and he pictured Reagan writhing in agony, basted alive by the hot torrent.

The hissing roar grew louder, then abruptly ceased as something made a hollow thump like a door closing, not far above.

Silence, taut and ominous, and the damp, neuter smell of cooling steam, broken by the urgent voice of Sanborn, calling out sharply even as he peered upward into the gray mass.

"Tip! Major Reagan! Foran! This is Colonel Sanborn! Speak up!"

Silence still, and hot steam thinning.

"Emergency! Colonel Sanborn to O.D.! Put me on intercom, all stations, fast!"

"Yes, sir." It was Lieutenant McPhee's voice. "Go ahead."

"Attention! This is Colonel Sanborn!"

Ike made himself speak slower and more distinctly as he heard the note of strain in his voice harshly amplified by the shaft speakers.

"All hands keep out of the main shaft above easy

deck! Technician Foran has run amok and attacked Major Reagan with the jet of a SCAT! The shaft is full of live steam from D-deck forward. Check your shaft air locks and report Foran on sight. Be careful!"

Sanborn stopped only to draw a breath.

"Captain Finberg and Duty Orderly, stand by your shaft door. Environment control, manifold for emergency suction on main shaft header and A-deck return lines, emergency pressure on F- and G-level shaft inlets as fast as you can! Cut in your auxiliary dehumidifier!"

The Colonel stopped and glared upward into the soggy gray mass. Foran or no Foran, he was not going to wait any longer to find out what had happened to Tip Reagan. Scowling, he sprang softly out along the catwalk to the stairs, conscious of the hot boiler-room smell of the air he drew into his lungs. Climbing with cautious speed, he had almost reached the catwalk at C-deck when he caught sight of Finberg poking a cautious head around the door marked "Med-Gym" and then stepping out quickly onto the landing. Big, blond Joe Alley was close behind. Sanborn opened his mouth to order them back until he had Foran spotted, but he was preempted by a call from overhead.

"Hey, Ike, you all right?"

The voice from the top of the shaft was unmistakably Reagan's!

The knot in Sanborn's stomach loosened, for it was

evident from Reagan's tone that he was not seriously injured, or, apparently, worried about another attack by Foran. Peering up the now visible but dripping corkscrew of the stairwell, he saw Reagan's head and shoulders leaning over the slanted rail high above. At the sight of Sanborn, the big Major gestured and started down. Obviously Foran was no longer a threat or Reagan would have been more cautious.

"Tip! Where's Foran?" Sanborn shouted back, squinting up apprehensively.

"Foran is over here, Commander," broke in Finberg from somewhere behind the titanium backbone of the ship. His tone was oddly quiet. "You'd better come look before we move him."

The grim implication of the doctor's words, emphasized by the even tone in which they were spoken, ran a cold finger down Sanborn's back, and he remembered abruptly and quite clearly the hollow thud with which the thruster's roar had ceased. A couple of steps along the catwalk disclosed what first the steam, then the big girders, had concealed from him. Foran, sightless eyes wide and looking very young and defenseless, was wedged into the angle between the shaft wall and one of the four big radial braces that jutted from the central shaft to form the basic skeleton on which C-deck was built. The sharp angle at which his head rested, and the little trickle of dark blood from a torn scalp that should have bled heavily, spelled broken neck to even a nonmedical person such as Sanborn.

Young Foran had found peace far quicker and more permanently that he had expected.

# 23

DEATH, especially unanticipated, pointless death, provokes an instinctive denial from the living, followed usually by a time of withdrawal. It was to be expected, therefore, that Foran's tragic and completely unexpected death would dim the bright glow of adventure that had imparted luster to even the simplest routine duties. People went about their tasks efficiently but mechanically, nor was their attitude affected by Dr. Finberg's statement that the broken neck that had killed Foran instantaneously had been followed by a skull fracture with resulting brain damage that would have reduced him to a human vegetable had he survived. Their quarrel was with the fact of Foran's death, not the circumstances, and time alone would disperse their resentful apathy.

Colonel Sanborn derived little comfort, too, from Finberg's diagnosis that the young astronaut had suffered from disorientation, a statement made only after intensive questioning of everyone aboard regarding any and all recollections of Foran's every word and action, right from the start of the trip.

"I'll never prove it now," said Finberg regretfully, "which is too bad because, if I'm right, the same thing could happen again to anyone whose geotropism is satisfied by the relative proximity of Earth during cislunar and lunar flight, but who may go to pieces in deep space. From what Aseto and Lin have told me I can almost guarantee that Foran suffered some sort of climactic attack during the repair flight to that cargo carrier. After this," he said as he rose to go, "I'll plan to be there when the repair craft comes in, if it's all right with you."

"Of course," assented Sanborn. "Anything —"

Beyond the normal sorrow and regret, the Commander couldn't rid himself of a sense of involuntary participation in the matter. It was not the first time he had been confronted by the fact of death, but it was the first time he might have prevented it. Had he taken the precaution of confining the suspects, Foran would be alive. The knowledge was bitter, the more so because he could not afford the luxury of time spent in regrets. As the party responsible for ultimate decisions aboard the *Pegasus,* he had done what he felt was best at the time, and he could not honestly fault his actions in retrospect. Nonetheless, Foran's life was part of the price he would always begrudge the red planet.

On instructions from Earth the body was frozen and sealed into one of three utility cases from the bionics compartment stores closet on C-deck. The case had stood on end in the rear of the closet. Seen flat on the floor on its side, there was no mistaking the contingent use for which it had been designed.

Fate decreed that Foran's physical remains should rest in the same box against which he had but recently braced himself to send the message that precipitated his final catastrophe. The ironic double encounter was not destined to trouble any human sensibilities, however, because the only one who would have recognized the grim jest was not talking — to anyone, ever again. By the time the hurriedly pocketed bit of microtape containing the message was found on the floor of his locker, the minutiae of George's itinerary were of interest to no one but Sims, who as security officer had to reconstruct the attempted hoax in order to furnish Sanborn, and the log, a written report.

When it came to planning a proper observance, Captain Spicer found himself torn between the duty to soothe and rekindle the living and the desire to say something profound, something that would give meaning to the seemingly meaningless death of a young man. After a decent interval he began questioning one after another of the astronauts, from Sanborn on down, harvesting recollections to add to his own meager knowledge of Foran.

Alone that evening with his store of impressions — George had left behind a unanimously vague image of a "nice kid" — Randy Spicer made a biographic outline of all he knew about the young astronaut in five minutes, then sat and stared at it for fifteen more, resenting the vast indifference with which an uncaring Destiny brushed a name off the roster of explorers, extinguishing dreams of fame and hopes of accomplishment even as they were beginning to take on substance. What do you say, he thought, to make that sound like anything but what it is, empty and disheartening.

". . . that we here highly resolve . . . shall not have died in vain . . ."

What was that? Out of a long-forgotten classroom exercise the words of Lincoln's austerely simple tribute on a far more difficult occasion came to mind, and Spicer clung to them, sensing in their somber dignity the strength and purpose he sought.

"But in a larger sense we cannot dedicate, we cannot consecrate, we cannot hallow this ground." The words came back with surprising ease. "The world will little note nor long remember what we say here . . ."

Spicer sat up straighter suddenly, perceiving in the great statesman's words the answer to his own problem and a rebuke to his sterile, resentful frame of mind. Who was he, after all, to demand a logical, human rationale for the inscrutable ways of the Almighty? And what was the matter with his faith in the Lord he professed to serve, that he should let himself be blinded to the needs of those he could help, by the selfish desire to make a memorable speech?

Leafing quickly through his Bible, he began scribbling notes to himself at the foot of the sheet of biographic data. Ps. 8, 3–4, he wrote, and Ps. 90, 2 and 4, in a sort of theological shorthand. When presently he sat back and slipped the sheet into his prayer book he was satisfied that he could speak meaningfully on the morrow.

His watch said nearly nine o'clock, time to put in his nightly appearance in the recreation room. This was an obligation he had fallen into the first night out from OFSET, when during a visit to the cola dispenser he had been called on to referee a roundhouse discussion of religion, faith, and God, occasioned no doubt by their departure on the interplanetary odyssey. Sensing an opportunity to open up new areas of interest and mutual understanding, he had soon had the group floundering enthusiastically about in the history and problems of the

Old Testament Israelites. By the time they had to call a halt to allow some to go on duty and others to bed, it had been agreed that there would be a nightly, one-hour meeting under the leadership of the Chaplain. Now in its second week, and showing no sign of petering out, the group bade fair to go on for another three or four weeks, possibly longer, exploring each other's personalities through the medium of the Book of Genesis, or Bereshith as Finberg's Masoretic text would read, from the Hebrew word meaning "In the beginning. . . ."

The death of young Foran, however, was the sort of thing that could put an end to the gatherings just when they could be of the most help, and Spicer expected to have his work cut out for him in getting the discussion off dead center. If there's anyone there to work on, he thought, heading out the door.

At the other end of the passage a figure emerged into the tiny foyer before the main shaft air lock, coming from the other narrow hallway that led to the quarters of Colonel Sanborn, Rowe, McPhee, Pryor, and Munn. It was the Exec, Major Reagan, later than usual tonight in concluding his visit with the Commander. The left leg of his slacks, Spicer noted, had an overstuffed appearance, and he remembered someone saying that the Major hadn't escaped completely unscathed from his encounter in the shaft.

"Wait up, Major," he called. "Are you going to join us? If there's anyone to join, that is —"

Reagan was almost always among those present to begin the nightly discussions but he never stayed more than a few minutes because he was acting-C.O. after seven o'clock. Now he looked around at the Chaplain with an odd little smile.

"They'll be there, Father," he said quietly. He always addressed Spicer as Father; it was a part of his Roman Catholic heritage. "There's a comfort in being together when the Dark One has passed by." As they started down the shaft he answered Spicer's original question. "Yes, I'll be stopping for a few minutes. Tonight," he added obliquely, "you'll be doing most of the talking, I think."

The Chaplain found Reagan's Celtic intuition to be right on both counts. The six or eight regulars were augmented by as many more, all sitting or standing about the far end of the recreation room in little clots of two or three, talking in low tones that ceased as soon as they saw him. It was obvious, both from the silence and from the look of quiet expectancy in the glances that met his, that they were all waiting for him to make some sense out of the senseless thing that had happened.

Walking to his inflated armchair set in the angle made by the side wall and the hull, he searched his mind for some appropriate way to break the silence and to shift the focus from Foran's death back to the living. Then, as he sat down, it came to him, the recollection of another evening not yet a week gone, when Foran had been present.

"Remember the night we talked about the idea of prayer?" he began quietly. "We got onto it from the story of the Garden of Eden and the concept of man talking with the Almighty. Someone said that it was ridiculous to teach a man he could get individual special treatment under the laws of the universe by talking to himself. Someone else said he'd agree with that if the first speaker could guarantee that whoever made those universal laws was not able to control their operation."

The original discussion had been a volatile one, and the Chaplain went on for a few minutes, recalling the wide-ranging thoughts that had been expressed. Then he paused — a smile of warm reminiscence lighting his big, homely features.

"He came up to see me afterwards," he said. No one looked in the least puzzled by the indefinite pronoun. "He asked me to excuse him for showing up so late. Said he was too embarrassed to say anything in front of the group. He thought I'd like to know that until that evening, he had always felt more or less as did the man who thought prayer was nonsense, but now he saw that maybe that was a pretty immature attitude in some ways.

He said he hadn't prayed since he was a kid but he was going to, that night, to thank God for the fact that the thing he wanted most out of life, to be a member of the first expedition to another planet, had come true. 'Padre,' he said to me, 'some people have to work and wait all their lives and maybe even then their dreams don't come true. Well, I've got mine, right here, right now, and that's a miracle when you think how many people tried out for the mission.'

"I'm not so sure it wasn't, now."

Spicer shifted in his chair, then added softly, "I've known people who lived a lot more years and whose dreams got pretty tattered and smudged before they were compromised or forgotten."

In the silence that followed, he knew he had done right to heed his intuition and relate the incident, for the dull, baffled resentment in their eyes had softened in the beginnings of acceptance and understanding.

# 24

IKE SANBORN immersed himself in the detail of the ship's daily routine to break loose from the leaden inertia that weighed on his spirits. He donned a radiation suit and took part in an overhaul of the power plant. He followed Lieutenant Ferris through the steps of an astral sextant reading. He even staged an unscheduled outer-hull inspection, performed by himself with Captain Larsen at the A-C's controls, guiding the small craft slowly around the great barrel of the spaceship while Sanborn peered at the antennae, sensors, hatch covers, strobe-light fixtures, attitude jets, all the breaks in the smooth outer skin of the *Pegasus*.

As they drifted gently back toward the recovery port, Sanborn could see, off to one side of their line of flight, the reddish gleam of a good sized star, brighter and bigger than any of its neighbors. Its size and location left no doubt of its identity.

"Mars," he said, without turning his head.

"Yes," replied his companion.

The apathetic mood of the astronauts showed little sign of change. People went about their business efficiently enough but without that air of suppressed enthusiasm that had marked the first part of the voyage. Sanborn recalled the closing words of General Charles's speech and, worried, sought the advice of Major Cardoza and Captain Finberg, both of whom assured him that the withdrawn air of the men would vanish in the face of any valid demand on their abilities. Nothing occurred to break the spell, however.

The ship's velocity was diminishing now at the same foot-and-a-half-per-second rate that had pushed it to over a million miles an hour, the fastest by far that most of those aboard had ever traveled.

"Of course the figure is empirically meaningless," said Lieutenant Lin, discussing their maximum attained velocity with Captain Ferris, Colonel Marcus's assistant. "One looks out the port or at the scanner and nothing seems to move. The mild linear acceleration, being less than a standard gravity and coinciding with our vertical axis, produces no sensory awareness of motion. Beyond that, our scale of miles per hour is ridiculously small for the measurement of planetary and stellar intervals."

Ferris, himself holder of a doctorate in astrophysics, knew as well as Lin that the scale was not even used in the disciplines concerned, where miles or kilometers per second, astronomical units, light years, and parsecs were the accepted measures of speed and distance. But he also knew that Lin was rather lonely a good share of the time because his pedantic manner of speaking and his inherent reserve cut him off from many of the others. Being of a similar nature, Ferris knew something of the compulsive urge to talk with someone that prompted Lin to make conversation almost pointlessly. He took only a sip from the cup he had been about to drain.

"You're quite right," he replied seriously. "I suppose that in time people will become conditioned to thinking of translunary distances in kilometers or miles per second instead of per hour. Our top speed was only a little over three hundred miles per second, which is roughly one-sixth of one percent of the speed of light. It is also about twice the angular momentum of the solar system about the hub of our Milky Way galaxy. There, by the way, is a larger yardstick for you — a galactic year."

Lin's bright black eyes gleamed, and Ferris could see the wheels turning as the former figured out the size of that monstrous unit: two hundred twenty thousand light years in circumference at the Earth's distance from the galactic center, and over two hundred fifty million earth years in duration at the speed the solar system is moving, better than a half million miles an hour.

"But —" expostulated Lin, "that yardstick is as much too big as the other was too small!"

"Quite so," laughed Ferris, "or perhaps we haven't evolved far enough to do more than peek through the keyhole of our little door on the cosmos yet. Right now, though," he went on, rising, "I'd better go get ready to take a sighting on Horeb for my boss at ten o'clock, or he'll have some crack to make about my lack of responsibility. I hope just once before this expedition is over he makes a human error, just a little one but a human error, so I can be sure he is human.

"Don't misunderstand me, Henry, I have the greatest admiration for the man's ability. If anyone has an intuitive grasp of astrophysical phenomena, it's Marcus, but that supercilious attitude of his gets to me."

He hurried from the room, followed by Lin's sympathetic smile. Marcus was not an easy man to have aboard, let alone to serve under.

This brief exchange took place three days after Foran's accidental death. It represented the first nonessential, spontaneous conversation beyond the simple civilities of greeting and parting and, of course, speculation about the tragedy. It proved to be the first crack in the wall of silence. By the next day, people were talking as freely as ever, their tongues helped along perhaps by the fact that that day marked their closest approach to the planet Venus.

Colonel Sanborn stopped at the Recreation Room on his way back from lunch to see what the nearby planet would look like to the unaided eye. The room was darkened, its occupants talking in low tones about the small, brilliant crescent that the *Pegasus,* traveling ten miles for every mile that Venus went, was overhauling at two hundred twenty miles per second. Right away the Colonel caught the note of spontaneity that had been missing for days, and he held back a sigh of relief as he moved quietly down the room toward the long plexite viewport. Halting behind the wide couch that fronted the window, he could just see the sharp sliver, like a tiny new moon, above the lower edge of the transparent plastic. Its relative motion made it appear to be creeping upwards against the background of stars.

Just then one of the shadowy figures on the couch spoke.

"When you think that that thing is moving in the same direction we are, at twenty-two miles per second, it gives you some idea how fast we're going to see it moving visibly in the opposite direction. It looks like a miniature moon rising, doesn't it?"

The voice was that of Ned Thomas, and he was

answered at once by John Pryor from a vantage point at one end of the viewport.

"That's right," he agreed, "but this moon keeps rising straight up, which bothers my terrestrial instincts; I keep expecting it to curve over and go back down."

Lieutenant Munn, whose black hair and skin made him nearly invisible in the darkened room, spoke up.

"You wonder what a man like Einstein would have come up with if he had seen something like this."

"Funny," observed Andy Lane, the expedition's other medic, "or maybe it isn't, under the circumstances, but I was just wondering the same thing about Leonardo. He knew the astronomy of his day and predicted that man would fly out into space." Lane thumped the couch beside him. "What do you suppose he'd say if he were sitting here now?"

" 'Who put out the lights?' probably," chuckled Munn.

Reassured by the banter, Sanborn, believing himself unobserved, started to turn away just as Pryor addressed a question to him over Thomas's head.

"How long will it be, sir, before we land on that one?"

"That depends on what you have in mind, Mister Pryor," replied Sanborn. "We can put a man on Venus, with very little risk, any time we wish. At present there is not enough to be gained, over what we can get from unmanned instrument landings and manned orbital survey craft, to justify landing a man. If you're thinking of an expedition like this one, our technology is not up to it yet. Venus is not a hospitable planet, you know, not like our current destination."

The Commander thought about his remark more than once in the next few days, wondering whether he had been rash to use the word hospitable in reference to the world that awaited them. That world, glowing a lurid orange-red, would be their home for the next five months, and now it was getting brighter and larger each day. The south polar cap swelled from a minute light spot on a ruddy marble to a glistening rough circle of white whose ragged edges, magnified on the scanner, revealed high, snow-drifted plateaus cut into by dark valleys and bounded by rolling hills. The hills were thickly stripped with impact craters, ranging from giant blast holes thirty miles and more in diameter down to dimples too small for the scanner to resolve. The snow cap had attained little of its winter growth as yet but the haze was thick above it and the night temperatures must be plummeting to below the $-200°$ mark on the Fahrenheit scale.

The expedition's landing area had been chosen in the northern hemisphere, not far above the equator, and timed for late spring to take advantage of the harsh environment's best weather. A year of 687 days, each one 24 hours 37 minutes long by terranean standards, meant a summer twice the usual length for the colonists, an attractive prospect until one learned that the temperature seldom reaches 75° Fahrenheit on the hottest equatorial noon and descends to −100° or lower at night. At a mean distance of 141.5 million miles from the sun, the planet receives but four-ninths as much solar radiation as does the Earth. It has no great oceans to serve as thermal reservoirs, and its tenuous atmosphere contains almost no water vapor to form clouds that would slow the nighttime heat loss by reverse radiation as they do on Earth. At its very best, Mars is no shirtsleeves paradise.

Then there are the winds and the dust, the all-pervasive, abrasive, microscopic dust. In summer the winds are light, sometimes ceasing altogether for a few hours, and seldom scouring up the choking, red-brown clouds. But in winter the thin wind wails an endless lament, flinging aloft a vast, dun dust shroud. The finest particles of this dust are so light that the weak gravity, only a third that of Earth, does not overcome the dispersing effect of the wind, and the shallow troposphere is saturated with invisible grit. Fatal to machinery, the dust helps to cut off the sun's ultraviolet rays, save during those rare days when eolian motion all but stops and gravity has its way. When that happens men must don their radiation shields to spend more than a few minutes outdoors.

# 25

Mars was a massive darkness obscuring the bottom of the starry void that was the scanner when at last the *Pegasus* slid up behind the mini-moon, Phobos, the ninety-six cargo sleds trailing in two long files.

Much as he wanted to get on with the landing on the planet itself, Sanborn welcomed the break provided by the visit to Phobos because it gave all hands a chance to let down briefly before the critical business to follow.

Reaching out a long, slim laser finger, the *Pegasus* tested the velocity of Phobos while all hands prepared for the approaching spell of zero gravity. Once the two speeds were equal, off would go the actinic drive and the ship would be swung slowly about to face forward, ready to accelerate to the higher orbital velocity needed when they moved closer to the surface of Mars.

On the Bridge, Captain Hewes looked up at one of the small video screens, watching a readout of the time to power cutoff. One hand grasped the re-rigged handline in anticipation of the return to weightlessness. For the same reason Lieutenant McPhee, at the master control console, and Technician Wood at auxiliary systems were firmly anchored to their seats by padded straps, their attention riveted to the banks of instruments that were the heartbeat and brain-wave monitors of the ship.

"Stand by for power cutoff in thirty seconds," announced McPhee over the intercom, alerting the crews that waited in various parts of the craft. As he finished, the air lock to the main shaft opened to admit Commander Sanborn, who moved quietly to the cargo carrier monitor and slid unobserved into the seat fastened to the deck behind it.

On the scanner the rim of the planet below had become discernible as two downswept streaks of vague luminosity that would have joined in the middle but for the intervening black bulk of Phobos.

"Fifteen seconds to cutoff."

The thin curve of dawn brightened fast now, turning from pink to tangerine to blood red almost before the final words of the countdown had ceased.

The change to weightlessness was only gradually apparent to their senses, for the difference in weight was small.

Thinking ahead to sunrise, Hewes was reminded of the old aphorism, "Red sun in the morning, sailors take warning." They would have to devise a new one for Mars, he mused, for the sun always rose red here.

"Permission to eject for Phobos." The words rasped out in Tandy's voice from the intercom. "Colonel Marcus wants to start now, to get there as soon as possible." Tandy, Marcus, and Mayer were waiting in an A-C, ready to set out for the landing.

In the back of the room the Commander smiled humorlessly. He had more or less expected the self-important Marcus to try to bend the schedule to his own advantage. Now, as McPhee turned questioningly toward his superior, Sanborn spoke.

"Everything on schedule, Captain?" he inquired firmly, as McPhee was about to speak.

Hewes, who had not heard the Commander come in, looked around in surprise. Both the question and the tone were unlike Sanborn, but the Captain wasn't slow to sense the reason.

"Yes, sir," he replied crisply.

"Fine! Let's keep it that way."

The Colonel looked right at McPhee as he said it, and that astute young man, waiting to ask if he should allow

Tandy to give Marcus his early start, perceived that he had the answer, almost grinned, and turned back to the console.

"Sorry, Amos. You're not due to leave until sunrise, another three minutes. We have to stick to the schedule, you know," he added for the benefit of Marcus, for whom both the trite acquiescence to authority and the blind acceptance of that authority as binding would be as salt in his wounded self-esteem. "Commander's orders," he added with a sophomoric solemnity that nearly ruptured the carefully correct expression of disappointment Tandy had assumed for Marcus's benefit.

The aggressive egalitarianism of Colonel Marcus in matters outside the scope of his own cluster of disciplines was recognized and tolerated by the rest of the crew, as was his arbitrary insistence that he be accepted as the sole authority on those matters within his competence. This was a prerogative of genius, and one that Sanborn tried to bend with when he was certain the situation would allow it. When, therefore, sunrise was but a minute away and Phobos moved into open sunlight, he caught Mc-Phee's eye and nodded.

"Let 'em go," he said, with a faint twinkle.

A moment later they saw the bright shaft of the A-C's rocket exhaust stab briefly at the darkness near the edge of the scanner's field of view. Then there was only the blip of the tracking beam's echo, dwindling imperceptibly as the little ship receded. Wood, at the scanner controls, narrowed the field to the immediate area of the A-C, and they could see the white cones of its landing lights feeling about for a flat spot, the overlapping circles of light shrinking as Tandy drew closer to the surface of the hurtling mountain range, over which dawn was flowing toward them.

Phobos had been a small black bug creeping across the ruddy face of Mars when viewed from a million miles away at high magnification. Close up, it was an awesome mass of bare rock, roughly ten miles thick, that completely filled the scanner screen even at low magnification. Now, as Wood panned slowly across its desolate face, the scene was an endless succession of bare cliffs, crater-pocked ledges and slopes, and depressions containing a few big boulders and a scattering of smaller detritus. Microid erosion and meteoric impact had blunted the lines and angles of the ancient crypto-satellite until the overall impression was one of immutable, timeless existence rather than one of great age.

Sanborn braced himself in the monitor seat, subconsciously adjusting to the weightless environment, and watched without any feeling of excitement as the auxiliary craft prepared to put down. He knew he should be stirred by this first human landing on Phobos, and so he was, in an abstract, spectator kind of way that was mostly technical appreciation of the accomplishment. Impatience, he realized, was his most noticeable feeling at the moment, a nagging urge to be about the expedition's real business.

"We're down," announced Tandy in a noncommittal tone that betrayed his pride in making the historic landing.

Colonel Marcus, on Tandy's right, was hampered by no such reticence. Marcus was unstrapped and fidgeting while the automatic landing system was still hissing and puffing to persuade the A-C to stay put on the surface in the almost nonexistent grip of Phobos's .001 gravity.

"Can't you hurry it up, Lieutenant?" inquired the astrophysicist ungraciously. "I have little enough time as it is."

Tandy, aware of the basic truth of the other's statement, replied with a cool affirmative and turned the landing system's sensors to their most insensitive setting. This had the effect of allowing the craft to teeter slightly without triggering a reaction from the ACS thrusters. Like a swimmer at neutral buoyancy trying to get both feet to rest on bottom, the little craft felt the rocks beneath it with one pad, then another, in a barely perceptible toe dance.

That's got it, nearly enough, decided Tandy, securing his suit and helmet while Mayer did likewise. In less than five minutes enough air had been exhausted from the small cabin to permit the impatient Marcus to pull back the hatch plate. Reaching out, he clipped his safety line to one of the O-rings and shoved himself through the hatchway, fumbling at his belt with the other end of the line. His abrupt movements tilted the nearly weightless A-C up on its two offside legs and would have tipped it over had not the attitude control jets squirted equally abruptly to counter the motion. The Colonel, unconcerned by the confusion he had instigated, set out for an upthrusting ledge some fifty feet away.

Sanborn, watching the scene on the scanner, was reminded of nothing so much as a gas-filled balloon by the way in which the white-suited Marcus rose in the air, hesitated, then sank back to the surface at each deliberate step. Was the anticipated powdery film really there, rising in a small cloud at each ponderous bootfall?

"Colonel, you forgot to attach the safety line to your belt!"

It was Tandy, calling after the departing scientist who, if he heard, paid no attention to the admonition. Perceiving this, Colonel Sanborn looked grim and almost cut in on the voice channel. Then he thought, no, this is perhaps the moment of a lifetime for him. If his theory of the asteroidal origin of Phobos and Deimos proves out, his name will be associated with the discovery for as long as the fact is considered worth propagating, probably for centuries. Anyway, he probably didn't even hear what Tandy said.

Such complete imperviousness was entirely in keeping with the degree to which Colonel Marcus could and did subordinate the sensory and practical aspects of his life to those of the objective scientific observer. More than anyone else Sanborn had ever met, this brilliant young man was an entity unto himself, rigorously suppressing his own feelings and ignoring his surroundings when they might come between him and his work, and almost childishly critical of other people's demands on his time and attention.

Again Tandy spoke, this time to Mayer.

"There may be something the matter with his helmet set. You'd better put on a backpack and go after him. Hook on another safety line; he's beyond the reach of the first one already."

"Yes, sir."

With surprising agility in one so large, Mayer slipped into the backpack the Lieutenant held out for him, then hopped out and attached a second hank of safety line to the free end of the one dangling outside.

It was during that moment that Colonel Marcus unintentionally initiated a sequence of events that was destined to change the views of a number of people, including himself. Reaching the foot of the ledge he had set out for, he examined what he could see of its fifteen-foot high face for igneous or sedimentary striation or other evolutionary signs but found only a vertical wall of the same dark, homogeneous basalt on which he stood. Having in mind to obtain a greater field of view, he glanced up at the flat top of the ledge, some nine feet or so above his head, flexed his knees and — unaccountably, thoughtlessly — jumped for it, with a result that he would have been the first to predict if asked. The Colonel kept right on going!

The tenuous gravity of Phobos did absorb some of his momentum, yet enough remained so that he seemed destined to float off on some sort of elliptic course, headed for empty space.

Fear provoked Marcus's second spontaneous reaction. Opening his mouth, he cried out in a very unscientific tone of alarm.

"Help! I'm floating away!"

Mayer was quickly on his way to the Colonel's aid. Even so, the burst of hoots, howls, and wisecracks that greeted this call for help on *Pegasus* might have seemed singularly callous to anyone who didn't know Marcus. The normally humorless Lieutenant Ferris, Marcus's assistant, treated himself to a gleeful grin. In the navigation compartment, where there was an open voice channel to the outside party, the only sound was Tandy's admirably neutral notice to Marcus that rescue was on its way. There were also four grins but these, of course, made no noise.

Wood, operating the scanner ranging control, zoomed

in on Marcus in time to catch his rescuer in the act of steering him down to the surface of the satellite, where they landed close to the Colonel's point of departure and to the loose end of the safety line Mayer had stretched out and dropped there. As the two cumbersome figures settled to the bare rock, Captain Hewes glanced back at Sanborn and murmured, "I'll bet Marcus could chew ice cubes and spit steam about now."

"Yes," agreed Sanborn, abruptly sorry for the brilliant younger man, for whom the landing on Phobos was probably the high spot of the entire voyage. Technical findings would not be affected, of course, but Marcus's recollections of the incident were bound to be less than pleasant.

Mayer must have shared the Commander's feelings, for now he spoke.

"This must be a big occasion for you, sir. I'd be glad to gather a random mineral sample, if it would help. That way you'd have more time to look for special things. Here —" Mayer unhooked his own coiled-up safety line from his belt and fastened one end to the spare. "I can't use this with a backpack unit, and it will give you a hundred-and-fifty-yard radius." Mayer fell silent and held out the other end of the line.

For an instant his companion did not move. It was like one of those suddenly arrested action pictures where the participants hang in frozen immobility. Colonel Sanborn found himself holding his breath, admiring Mayer's courage as much as his thoughtfulness. Marcus had the rank, and now the excuse, to salve his wounded pride by giving Mayer a verbal flaying for a half-dozen petty offences against the code of conduct expected of enlisted men, offences such as offering unsolicited advice and opinions to an officer, speaking out of turn, and so on. Figuratively hunching his shoulders, the Commander waited for the blast.

Deliberately Marcus reached out and took possession of the safety line, but made no move to attach it to his belt. Softly, almost thoughtfully, he began to speak.

"It has been several years since a technician, civilian or military, has thought it advisable to instruct me in the performance of my work. But then, I dare say you knew that, did you not, Mister Mayer?"

"Yes, sir," replied the bigger man quietly.

"I am not unaware, you see, of my reputation for a sharp tongue, a reputation that I have been at some pains to foster. It has saved me many hours, hours that were put to better use. I suspect you never thought of it from that point of view, did you, Mister Mayer?" Marcus's voice was slightly louder and his words came a bit faster than before.

"Not exactly, sir," acknowledged the other.

Listening closely, Sanborn was still not sure what Marcus was about. He frowned grimly, hoping that the irate Colonel would keep in mind that he had five more months to spend with this little band of men, most of whom were watching and listening to his present remarks.

After a barely noticeable hesitation, Marcus continued, restraint lending a harshness to his inflection.

"Thank you for saving me from the consequences of my own errors in judgment. Had I put on my safety line to begin with or heeded the Lieutenant's warning, there would have been no need for you to come to my rescue. I shall welcome your assistance, in the spirit in which it was offered. Do you know how to use these?"

"These" were a sample bag and tongs, in sterile plastic envelopes, which Marcus pulled from his belt clip and held out to his companion.

"Yes, sir, I do," answered Mayer with alacrity as he took the collecting kit.

"Good! Get me three or four small stones from each of those dips." Hooking the line to his belt, Marcus pointed. "Then two or three from that big impact crater the other side of the A-C. And hurry, because I'm sure the Commander and the rest are as anxious to get on with their assignments as I was to get here," concluded the scientist in a tightly determined, determinedly cheerful tone, moving cautiously away.

Back aboard the *Pegasus,* Lieutenant Ferris couldn't make up his mind whether he was really glad that his self-centered boss had at last made a mistake or sorry that

Marcus's comeuppance had been so public. Certainly the Colonel must have been quite humbled, knowing as he did that the entire crew was looking and listening. The incident might well dog him the rest of his life, something to be brought up again and again by jealous colleagues with smooth smiles of derision. In the end, though, Ferris decided he was glad it had happened. His superior officer had been a pretty obnoxious character at times and deserved his lesson. Too, there was something about the way Marcus had handled himself afterward that left the young Lieutenant with the feeling that perhaps the lesson had been learned, at least in part.

On the bridge a momentary silence greeted the end of Marcus's remarks. Wood, as the only noncommissioned officer present, reserved his impressions for a more opportune moment. McPhee, a coolly objective young man, decided that Marcus might live to grow up emotionally after all, and he was faintly surprised to sense that he was personally relieved that Mayer had not gotten chewed out for his thoughtfulness.

Captain Frank Hewes was the first to break the silence. Without looking away from the screen, on which Marcus bobbed sluggishly about his stony obstacle course, the captain spoke in a tone of quiet disbelief.

"There is a man I misjudged, Ike. I thought sure he was going to burn Mayer to a cinder! That little speech took some doing, especially since he knew everyone on board was looking on."

When the Commander did not reply, Hewes glanced over at him, then turned for a closer look. Sanborn, too, was staring at the screen, a lopsided, happy grin turning up one corner of his big mouth.

"Never too old to learn, Captain," he acknowledged finally, returning Hewes's stare with one that seemed compounded of equal parts chagrin and satisfaction. "I thought so too, and I was sitting here worrying over what he was going to do to our morale and team spirit. Mayer, God bless him, just made his speech and stood there, holding out the safety line, and Marcus took it." Sanborn smiled as if that explained everything, then went on in response to Hewes's questioning look. "Thanks to Mayer, who had the courage to be compassionate, Marcus has found not only his precious mineral samples on that for-saken rock pile but something of greater value. He has found that there is something within himself which de-mands a greater allegiance even than his profession — his self-respect and integrity as a human being — and I think he knows now that he can't have that without respecting it in others."

Turning back to the white-clad figures on the screen, Ike was suddenly impatient again, eager to get to the real business of the expedition, the landing and settlement at *Lunae Palus.*

"That's a good omen," he said enthusiastically. "A man with the courage to be compassionate and another man with the guts to admit his mistakes and get on with the job. Who better to settle a new world!"

# Glossary of Space Terms

*These definitions are included only as an aid to a clearer comprehension of the text. Many of them are neither exhaustive nor professionally phrased.*

ACCELERATION   A change in the rate of motion of a body. Linear acceleration means a constant, unvarying acceleration, rectilinear or curvilinear.

ACTINIC DRIVE   A propulsion system powered by light.

ALGAE   A plant of any of various classes containing chlorophyll, such as the seaweeds.

ALPHANUMERIC KEYBOARD   A keyboard containing the usual numeric digits 0 through 9 plus letters of the alphabet used as digits to make a numbering system of larger scope than the decimal one.

AMBIENT PRESSURE   The pressure prevailing at the time and place in question.

ANGSTROM   A scale of measurement used to define the length of energy waves. Defined variously as one ten-millionth of a millimeter or one hundred-millionth of a

[ 2 1 5 ]

centimeter (the same thing), it is abbreviated A. and carries the symbol λ, the Greek letter *lambda*. Its use is commonly confined to wavelengths running from infrared, at 10,000, A., down to so-called "hard" X rays at as little as a thousandth of an A. An Angstrom filter is a device that passes only predetermined light wavelengths.

ASTRAL    Relating to the stars.

ASTRONOMICAL UNIT    The smallest of the commonly used astrophysical yardsticks. It is 93,000,000 miles, the mean distance from the Earth to the sun.

BINARY    Composed of two parts, a pair, double.

CISLUNAR    This side of the Moon. See Ultralunar.

CONSOLE    A control and/or instrument panel.

CRYPTO-SATELLITE    An extremely small satellite. Both Martian satellites are less than ten miles in diameter, as contrasted with our Moon's thickness of over 2000 miles.

CRYSTAL EMITTER    An energy transmitter, part of the hypothetical Kresch drive.

DECELERATION    Slowing down, negative acceleration.

EMISSION LINES    Bright vertical bars in the color band of an emission spectrum.

EMPIRIC    Experienced through the senses, as opposed to rational, derived through reason.

ESCAPE VELOCITY    In orbital mechanics, the speed at which a body must move to escape the gravity of its home planet. Earth's escape velocity is seven miles per second.

GEE    An acronym for the normal sea-level gravity that will cause a falling body to accelerate at just over 32 feet per second.

GEOCENTRIC    Having the Earth as a center, as does the Moon's orbit.

GIMBALS    A device that allows spherical motion by means of a mounting permitting circular motion, itself mounted on a piece that permits circular motion at right angles to the first mounting.

GYRO    Gyroscope or gyroscopic device.

HELIOCENTRIC    Having the sun as a center.

HOLOGRAPHIC    An information storage and recovery system utilizing three dimensions to record much more information on a tape than is possible using only two dimensions.

HYDROPONIC STATION    A place where vegetable foods are grown without soil by immersing their roots in chemically treated water.

IN VACUO    In a vacuum.

INERTIA    The force that tends to keep a motionless body at rest and a moving one going without change in speed or direction.

INFRARED    A band of wavelengths of electromagnetic energy just longer than the longest visible light waves. The heat we feel in sunlight is conveyed to us by infrared waves.

INTERLOCK    A safety device intended to prevent acts from taking place in improper sequence.

IRRADIATOR    A device for producing or focusing radiation.

KRESCH DRIVE    A hypothetical actinic drive, a name chosen at random by the author.

LASER    Light Amplification by Stimulated Emission of Radiation.

LIGHT YEAR    An empirically inconceivable distance, about six trillion miles, beside which a journey to the Moon is as a grain of sand beside Mount Everest.

MEGAWATT    A million watts.

MICROTAPE    Recording tape on which the bits of information, tiny magnetized spots, are very small and close together.

MILLIGEE    A thousandth of a standard gravity.

ORBIT    The path followed by one body moving as a satellite about another body. The planets move in elliptical orbits about the sun.

OXIDIZER   In rocketry, the substance (LOX, peroxide, etc.,) that provides the oxygen needed for combustion.

PICOTORR   A trillionth of a torr. See Torr.

PITCH   A longitudinal see-saw motion.

POSIGRADE   Forward.

POWER RING   Part of the Kresch drive.

RAY-CLASS SHIP   Hypothetical two- or three-man space-ship such as described in *Marooned in Orbit*.

ROLL   A sideways rocking motion.

SERVOMECHANISM   A device that performs a given function on signal, usually automatic.

SLURRY   A mixture of solids, liquids, and sometimes gases, that can be handled like a liquid.

SOLENOID   An electromagnetically operated lever.

STANDARD GRAVITY   Roughly, the Earth's sea-level gravitation, equal to an accelerated force of 32.2 feet per second.

STROBE LIGHT   A light that flashes electronically at high intensity for a small fraction of a second.

TELEMETRY   Transmission of data by microwave signals in patterns controlled by automatic sensors.

TORR   A unit of vacuum measurement, one-seven hundred sixtieth of a standard atmosphere of roughly fifteen pounds per square inch. A thousandth of a Torr is called a "micron."

TROPOSPHERE   The thick bottom layer of Earth's atmosphere, five to six miles deep, under which we live.

ULTRALUNAR   Beyond the Moon, from Earth. See Cislunar.

VELOCITY   Speed, rate of motion.

VISCOSITY   In a fluid or plasma, thickness.

YAW   Turning motion, like a weathervane.